WHITE LIES

Skye Warren

CHAPTER ONE

Before

IT'S AN ABSOLUTE madhouse.

A woman juggles a baby and a toddler while a third, slightly older child, raids a supply closet with blankets and plastic urinals.

A man in a wheelchair with no legs hollers in the corner while the harried nurses bustle past him as if he's silent.

Stretchers full of moaning, injured people line the hallways, waiting for a room.

Even more ambulances arrive at the Emergency Room door.

We were lucky, if you could call it that. Being conked on the head gave Emerson a fast pass into the CT scan. It came back clear, so they're hoping to discharge him and make space for someone else.

I step into the night, where a parked ambulance flashes its lights, a soundless refrain.

The moon looms high and heavy. A full moon. That probably explains the excess of accidents in the hospital tonight. And at the circus. I wouldn't have given that idea any thought twelve months ago, but the circus is a superstitious lot.

They've rubbed off on me.

And I need some reason for the disaster we're facing.

Something to blame.

I pull out my cellphone and call Wolfgang.

The knife thrower answers on the first ring. "Sitrep," he says, revealing his time in the military, though he usually tries to hide it. Situation report.

"I have it on scientific authority that his head is hard as hell."

A pause, which is the most emotion we really ever get from the bastard. He's the least showy showman… at least until he has sharp metal in his hands. He's ex-military, which always struck me as interesting. The circus, with all its wild, haphazard ways seems like a strange path for someone who still operates like a soldier. Someone who's awake early for pushups and a ten-mile run every day, rain or shine. Then again, it has the camaraderie, the sense of a unit, that's rare in town life. Isn't that why I joined the circus? No, I came for a darker reason. But the feeling of family? That's why I stayed.

"Good," he says, his voice gruff.

"We're waiting on some meds, and then we should be discharged."

Another pause, this one less relieved. More tense. "You might want to take your time."

Unease has been swirling in my gut ever since I peeled away from the fairgrounds, mud slopping along the undercarriage of the truck, raindrops as fat as hail pelting the windshield. "What the hell's happening there?"

"You don't want to know."

Fuck. "Is it Alessandra?"

The brash, impetuous fortune teller is the reason we're in this mess. She's always starting drama with people in the circus, or worse, stirring up trouble in the towns we pass through. "Don't worry about it," Wolfgang says. "Just stay gone."

He ends the call.

I swear at the pock-marked moon.

A few lingering drops of rain land on my face in placid answer.

When I make my way back through the too-full emergency room, I find the small bay that holds Emerson's hospital bed already occupied. With a woman, of course.

"Here's my cellphone number," she purrs. "I get off my shift in an hour. I wouldn't want anything to happen to you, for you to be in any pain… I don't mind nursing you. Personally."

"What an enchanting offer," the ringmaster says in his usual fluid tones. "Though I wouldn't want to offend anyone with my presence. A lover, perhaps?"

A giggle. "My husband is a truck driver. He's been gone for four weeks."

"Too long to leave a sensual creature like yourself alone," he says with a heavy spoonful of sympathy. "Perhaps you're the one who's in pain."

Christ.

Even falling ten feet and slamming his head into the metal platform of the Ferris wheel doesn't slow him down from charming women. It's enough to make a man annoyed as hell, if I were actually interested in sex or dating. Which I'm not. When you have my blood running through your veins, it's safer for everyone if you stay away.

I push aside the heavy vinyl divider and clear my throat.

The nurse jumps. Her eyes widen at whatever she sees written on my face.

"Well," she says, in a bright, professional tone. "I'll let you guys get out of here but remember my written instructions. They'll make you feel *so* much better."

Then she's gone in a bustle of squeaky sneakers and scrub-fabric swishes.

I raise an eyebrow at Emerson.

He holds his hands palm up, expressive even when he's not commanding a crowd of revelers under the big top. "Can I help it if the nurses in this town are so exceedingly generous with their time? Natural born caregivers, every one of them."

"You're not going to visit her."

"*Naturellement.*"

"Because you don't fuck married women?"

"*Non.* Because I would not be able to perform up to my usual standards with this little head injury. My masculine pride could not withstand anything but turning a woman into a screaming, melting puddle of climax. Multiple times."

"I've seen the results of your masculine pride. The women who start hanging around the tent. Who demand to see you. I've had to escort a few off the fairgrounds."

"Is it my fault that I am so charming and so

skilled?"

"Honestly? Yeah."

A soft, soundless laugh. "Perhaps you're right. I live for the attention."

"You've had enough attention for the night. I'm needed back at the fairgrounds."

Hazy dark eyes close against the intruding reality. "What's she done now?"

"She better not have done anything. If she's even sneezed I'm going to lose it. I told her to stay in the fucking fortune teller's tent until I got back."

"I trust you aren't going to be too harsh on her."

That makes me pause in the act of handing him his dress shoes—once shiny, now streaked with dried mud. "What do you think I would do to her?"

Anyone else would flinch away from the question. Emerson only studies me with those dark mysterious eyes. "I could not begin to guess, *mon ami*."

Everyone knows who my father was. What he did. It was an open secret in the circus, even when he was wasted away and dying, being carted from city to city in a tiny trailer hitched to the back of someone's RV. There were no doctors or diagnoses. Only a frail old man, his tapestry of tattoos turned stretched and warped as he lost pound after pound.

I had to stoop to even set foot inside the trailer. The air was tinged with sickly sweet marijuana smoke. "Hello, Son," came the haggard voice from the mattress on the floor.

I shake my head, forcing myself back to reality.

"I would never hurt her."

"Ah," he says. "Some of the townie morality."

In the circus being a townie, someone who stays put, is an insult. "Yes, we prefer not to hit women or kick puppies. How provincial of us."

"Then she will only do it again." He touches a hand to his forehead, which is covered in a bandage. A lock of dark hair falls rakishly over the sterile white gauze. "It's the only way we ever learn anything. Through pain."

I give him a sardonic look. "What did you learn from the pain in your head?"

"Obviously I learned never to be gallant. I don't know what came over me, but I can assure you it won't happen again."

Tonight, the storm blew into Charleston with sudden intensity. The cracking thunder and driving rain sent most of the ticket holders away.

That would have been a major blow already, our income dashed for an entire night of work. The true danger, though, was the wind. It pulled the stakes from the newly wet ground and knocked our tents over. It knocked over a floodlight which started a small electrical fire in the largest tent, the big top. I'd been dealing with that when someone called me over to the Ferris wheel.

Apparently Alessandra had decided that taking a ride in the wild rain would be exhilarating. She wasn't wrong, precisely. Except the finicky equipment decided to break when she was near the top. It did that often, seeing as our mechanic was a drunk. Though more likely because the entire ride needed to be decommissioned.

Gerard Marino, the owner of Cirque des Miroirs, would not pay for that.

She'd been trapped up there as the wind had swung her wildly, back and forth, her shrieks of entertainment turning into panic. Emerson made it halfway up the slippery metal skeleton of the ride before a crack of lightning hit the entire structure.

The spark had knocked him off.

He landed hard on the metal platform.

I'd climbed up after him, quickly, even carelessly in my concern over both Alessandra and

Emerson's safety. I'd practically dragged the quivering fortune teller out of the car and handed her down to men who were gathered beneath to catch her.

Emerson could have died. Or been seriously injured.

It was only providence and probably part of the ringmaster's cat-like seven lives that let him walk away with a few scratches.

I drive back to the fairgrounds through an unfamiliar city. Unease weighs down my foot on the gas pedal, urging me to go faster, warning that something bad is happening. Something more than fire and a fall in the same night?

No wonder they're superstitious about full moons.

We arrive to a startling sight.

In two hours most of the circus could have been packed away, especially now that the worst of the storm has cleared, leaving an unholy light. It illuminates the abandoned fairgrounds, tents half submerged in mud, metal swings from the mechanical ride creaking faintly.

A hundred people should be out here working.

My jaw clenches. "I suppose it's too much to assume that Marino gave everyone the night off after so much already happened and he's going to let them pack up in the morning."

Emerson points toward the big top, which normally stands tall and proud. We pulled free one of the major supports while putting out the fire. It gives the large red-and-white striped tent a lopsided appearance, one half of it deflating like a balloon. Light peeks through the edges of the flaps, which means it's probably occupied. "I think you're about to see the most dangerous and daring show the Cirque des Miroirs has to offer."

"No one should even be inside the tent without the left support beam."

"Safety is never the goal in a circus."

"It damn well should be."

"And what would you suggest, townie?"

"I may have only been here a year, but even I can see that we need policies in place. A system for shutting down the circus in inclement weather. A policy for when to run the rides and when to stop, even if people want to keep riding. Hell, we should have a medic on staff."

A bark of laughter. Emerson immediately grabs his head, revealing that it hurt to do that. "I suppose you're going to convince Marino to pay for that, are you?"

"Are the pain meds wearing off?"

"It's not too bad. It could be worse. After all, I could be rolled into a ditch."

I don't look at him as I step out of the cab of the truck. Rolled into a ditch.

Emerson is one ballsy motherfucker, I'll give him that.

The day I came to a circus I asked to see The Freak Show, a man famous for his many colorful tattoos and piercings, a minor, outdated celebrity in the world of circus sideshows. After being shut down and threatened with violence if I didn't leave the premises, I caught the notice of the owner. Gerard Marino recognized me, because he's one of the few men who'd ever seen my father before he was covered from eyelid to eyelid with ink.

He'd let me inside to see my father.

In his weakened state it had been easy to convince him to tell me his crimes. In between hacking coughs and shudders of pain, he listed as many as he could remember, women he lured and then held down, possible babies he'd left all across the country for decades. Not a short list.

Then I'd picked up one of the blood-spittled rags and held it against his face.

He convulsed once, twice.

A third time, his eyes bulging.

And then he was silent.

He was the first man I ever murdered, but not the last.

It was retribution for my mother, who'd lived a sad, lonely life before cancer took her.

It was also, ironically, the price of entry into the circus.

Rather than call the cops on me, Marino had ordered me to hide the body. He told me he'd needed someone strong and decisive. I would do. So I rolled my father's distorted and wasted-away body into a ditch.

I walk toward the dimly lit, lopsided big top, my stomach clenched against whatever I'm going to see inside. I've heard stories, of course. Rumors. I hoped they were exaggerations. The way he made the clowns fuck each other for his own amusement when he felt like they weren't performing with enough enthusiasm. The time he forced a man into a cage with a hungry bear after he'd stolen money from the ticket stand. Ruthless. And cruel. That's his legacy.

I'm about to find out how much of it is true.

CHAPTER TWO

Present day

A THICK FOG descends over the fairgrounds. So thick it almost has a flavor, the loam and the clay of the earth turned into a fine mist. The equipment is mostly packed away, the circus working with subdued order in the wake of the storm. Not only the physical encounter. The scare. The risk. We aren't accustomed to danger anymore.

Sure, every trapeze act involves risk, but we minimize it with rigorous practice.

Our systems and procedures keep everyone safe.

A registered nurse moonlights as a costume designer, always available.

We don't have accidents anymore, until last

night. I've been calm and contained every show, every town since then. This night is different, because it reminds me of before.

I couldn't punish Sienna, not the way Marino would have.

So I did the only thing left to protect the circus: I sent her away.

Why does it feel like absolute bullshit?

I'm not a danger to the fucking circus. That's what Sienna told me.

It felt like the truth, even though I knew it to be a lie.

Should I have believed her? Maybe I would have if it had only been Albert. He's a good worker, but also a shit starter. Would Emerson lie about her? Maybe. No. I hope not, anyway. But even if I could have doubted them, I don't doubt Alessandra's daughter, Cat.

At least I never have until now.

The purple constellation-patterned fortune teller's tent is the only structure remaining. I ordered the men to leave it alone, like it's some kind of shrine to Sienna. Which is ridiculous. She wasn't even our permanent fortune teller. That has always been Alessandra, despite her absence these past few weeks. She's not quite reliable, but she always comes back.

Marino kept her around because she's an absolute expert at fleecing unsuspecting townies of their money. She can always cajole them into paying more for a special prediction from the pagan gods or even a spell designed to cast good fortune.

I keep her around for a different reason entirely.

Guilt.

No, this tent didn't belong to Sienna.

Nothing did, which is a knowledge that sinks in my gut.

She was alone in this world, battered and bruised by the men in her life. I could have been different. I *should* have been different, but somehow I failed her. Somehow I didn't realize she was going to take unnecessary risks. Somehow I didn't know she would climb that Ferris wheel in the storm, like Alessandra did all those years ago.

History repeating itself.

Soft footsteps approach the tent.

Cat peeks her head inside. "You asked to see me."

"Come in. Sit down." I gesture to the tufted bench that circus attendees use when they're having their tarot cards read. The cards themselves are in one of the compartments beneath the table, along with mystical-looking crystals, dried herb bundles, and a white powder that I don't even want to know what it is. These are the tools of the fortune teller. The props she uses to convince others of an illusion they want to believe in.

I'm no fortune teller.

I'm the owner of this circus. Someone determined to get to the truth.

Cat sits down, clearly uncomfortable, tucking her curly black hair behind her ear.

"How old are you now?"

She blinks. "Seventeen."

"Have you ever thought about leaving the circus?"

Her dark eyes widen, so like her mother's and yet so much more innocent. Not jaded. I've worked hard to make sure she doesn't have a reason to be. She starred in our first production of this show, the one I created based on Alice in Wonderland after I took over.

She was the young girl who climbed through the looking glass and discovered a world of amazement, her dark curls bouncing, her blue dress puffed up by layers of white ruffles. By the time she hit puberty she was already proficient with a cello, so we moved her to the band. The daughter of one of the butchers stepped in as the little girl in the show.

"What else would I do?" she asks.

It doesn't feel like an idle question. "Anything you want. You could settle down. Just because your mother prefers this life doesn't mean you have to."

Sorrow enters her eyes. "Have you heard anything about Mom?"

"No, I'm sorry I haven't," I say gently. "I have people looking for her."

She bites her lip. "I know she always comes back, but what if she doesn't? What if she's in jail or worse? What if she's hurt?"

I clear my throat against the guilt. "We'd know if she were in jail. North Security is the premiere private security firm in the country. Maybe even the world. They have contacts in law enforcement. And in morgues. There are no Jane Does matching her description."

Relief makes her slump. "I don't understand why she doesn't take me with her."

The woman goes on drug-fueled benders where she sleeps with men. Until she gets tired of them. Then she leaves them tied up in motel rooms and takes their money. It's one of the rare gifts Alessandra gave her daughter, not teaching her that part of her lifestyle. "I'm sure she wants what's best for you. Maybe you could get your GED. Go to college."

"And do what?" Her nose scrunches. "How to work in a bank? No, thanks."

A reluctant smile tugs at my lips. The circus life is addictive. People like Cat are born into it. Most never leave. They find some role in the circus. That role may change. Even the circus itself may change, though mostly people don't leave Cirque des Miroirs.

They never go back to town life.

"Caterina. I need to ask about what happened."

Her face turns white. "I told you about it already."

"No, you told Emerson. Who told me. I want to hear it from you."

Her hands twist together. "Well, like I said, she wanted to take a ride in the Ferris wheel. She kept saying it would be fun, but Albert said it wouldn't be safe. That we have systems in place for a reason. She said she'd prove him wrong by climbing herself."

"Had you ever seen her do anything like that before?"

"No, I mean, I've barely even talked to her.

Just brought her clothes and supplies when you asked me to. It's a big circus."

A big circus, but there are not that many women around their age. They could have been friends. Allies. "Were you afraid that she would take your mother's job permanently?"

Long dark lashes cover her eyes. "Maybe."

I lean forward. "Did this seem like a way to get rid of her?"

Panic flashes across her expression. "Yes. I mean, no. I mean, how could I lie about something like this? How could we all be lying?"

"That's a good question," I say, my voice turning hard. "If you're all lying with the same story, then it means it was premeditated. Collusion. I'm just not sure why you'd do it."

"I—I didn't do that."

"No? Then why is your pulse beating so fast?"

One tear slips down her cheek. "Please. Why are you treating me like this?"

A bark of laughter escapes me. "This? This is nothing compared to what the old owner of the circus would do. You don't remember him, do you? You were only a little girl when he left."

Her eyes meet mine. "I've heard stories," she whispers.

"They're all true," I say, my voice flat.

"You took the circus from him. That's what people say."

"That's right."

"I've always wondered—I always wanted to know—are you my father?"

The question sets me back a moment. "What?"

"The timing, my mother would never be clear. And people said you were together. That you were a couple for years. They even say that it's the reason why you…"

"They say it's the reason I took over the circus."

"Yes," she whispers again.

My voice goes soft. "I'm sorry. You're not my daughter."

She flinches. "Oh."

"I care about you, Cat. I care about everyone in the circus. You're like my family. The circus *means* family. If anything is ever scaring you, you can tell me."

"Can I?" Her voice is luminous, more mature than before. More reckless.

"Yes."

"I think if I tell you the truth you might be the thing that scares me. The kinds of things that people said Marino did… sometimes I wonder if you could do them too."

I give her a hard, bitter smile. "Yes. I have violence inside me, if that's what you're asking. You're going to tell me the truth anyway, though, Caterina, aren't you?"

Her eyes widen at my tone. "I—I did tell you the truth."

The truth. A funny concept considering I didn't believe Sienna only twenty-four hours ago. Refused to believe her. Was I blinded by the past? "Try again."

She shifts on the bench, a place where so many circus patrons have come—most to hear an entertaining bit of nonsense but some came to hear a desperate hopeful truth. "I don't know what you mean."

"I don't think it was your idea. I'll give you that much."

"Mr. Whitmere, please."

"Someone came and told you to do this. And you do what you're told, don't you?"

Tears slip down her cheeks. "No one was supposed to get hurt."

"Not like last time. But then, I suppose they didn't tell you about last time."

"What?"

"Never mind. Who told you to do this? Who

told you to lie to me?"

Her words come out in a hoarse whisper. "I wanted him to see me as a woman. I thought if I went along with it, if I proved to him that I was—"

"Who?"

"It was just supposed to be a… a white lie."

"Tell me who, goddamn you."

"Mr. Durand."

Emerson.

There it is. Proof that I've been betrayed by someone who's become my best friend over the years. Proof that I should have listened to my gut and trusted Sienna, despite the evidence.

Proof that she's been used, bullied, and mistreated one more time in her life…

And this time, I was the one who did it.

I thought you were different, she said to me.

I stand with enough force to shove the table a few inches in Cat's direction.

She also jumps up, looking frantic. "You aren't going to—"

"Aren't going to what?"

"You aren't going to fire Mr. Durand, are you?"

I bare my teeth in a facsimile of a smile. "I'm going to do a lot worse than fire him. And my advice to you, Caterina Gallo, is to worry about yourself. Because you betrayed the circus. And our beloved ringmaster sure as hell isn't worried about you."

CHAPTER THREE

Before

I'M STRIDING TOWARD the lopsided, lumpy big top.

My gut churns, not knowing what I'm going to find inside. Or how I'm going to stop it.

Emerson's hand grabs my arm.

"What?" I demand, swinging back to face him.

"You don't need to go in there. Come with me. Let's get drunk. Or we can meet up with that nurse. I bet she would like both of us in the room. Me charming her. You glaring at her. She would have the best night of her life."

"I don't fuck married women."

"Based on my observation, you don't fuck anyone."

Because I have darkness in my veins. My father held down women and hurt them all across the country and back again. That's what I came from. "I'm going in the tent."

He shakes his head and then winces at the movement. "There's nothing you can do to help her, if he's trying to set an example for everyone."

Set an example. With a woman. My skin crawls with the realization.

And the hint of sorrow in Emerson's dark eyes. This man is known to be calloused, even cruel. If he doesn't want to see what's happening in the tent, it's bad.

"This is fucking bullshit."

"It's the animal kingdom. Why do you think the bears and tigers know their place? Because they recognize who has the most power, who isn't afraid to use it. And for all that, he's a cold-hearted bastard, he's also the alpha of the pack."

A low sound escapes me, one of barely contained fury. "That's some real rich, gold-plated bullshit, you know that? We're not animals. We're people."

"I never fail to enjoy your commentary on circus life."

That's a thinly veiled reminder that I'm a townie, regardless of my job title. Nine months ago I had never worked in a circus. Most of these people? Not only have they worked for Cirque des Miroirs for years. Most of them were also born into the circus life.

It's a tradition passed down from mother to daughter, from father to son.

"Go fuck your pretty little nurse," I say, my voice rough. "Do whatever you want."

I head toward the tent, and he doesn't stop me this time. Despite his bravado I think he's too hurt to actually head back into town for a hookup, no matter how cute the RN was. More likely he's going to his RV to drink himself to oblivion, which is what I should be doing.

Instead, I push through the tent flap.

My feet stop in the mud, as if they weigh a thousand pounds.

Gerard Marino is twelve kinds of bastard, but he's also the closest thing to a father figure in my life. He took me on when I was wandering around, unable to settle down, because my heart, my body, my very soul needed to keep moving.

I need the circus.

Time slows as I reach the flap.

Blood pumps as thick and slow as the mud beneath my boots.

I push into the tent.

For a brief, suspended moment it looks like an ordinary rehearsal, someone high in the air while others gather around with encouragement.

It's what I want to see, a mirage. Not real.

Then the picture comes into terrible focus.

The person suspended on one of the trapeze bars isn't an acrobat. It's Alessandra. Something thin and black flies through the air. A whip. The animal trainer, a woman named Janie, doesn't actually use it on the animals. She flicks it as an extension of her own arm, to gesture to the animals, for showmanship.

She's standing with her arms wrapped around herself, her skin pale, looking up.

One of the few who are looking up.

Most of the people have their eyes downcast. Or they stare straight ahead.

This is a lesson in endurance.

Marino stands in the center of the ring, still wearing a drenched suit, his white dress shirt turned brown from the mud—flecked with darker spots.

Alessandra's blood.

Without pausing, I stride to the center of the ring. Fury burns in my stomach. Red blinds me. I never wanted to be the violent man my father was, but now I understand. It's been there all along, the dark impulses. To hold down, to control. To ruin. "What the fuck are you doing?"

Marino's breath smells like whiskey, but his eyes are clear enough. Not drunk. Just fucking evil. "Showing you what the circus is really about, boy. You didn't think it was all pony rides and popcorn, did you?"

I force myself to take a breath. One, then another. "Stop this," I say, my voice low.

We're standing in front of everyone. There's no real way for him to save face, but I'll be damned if I let this continue. I keep my gaze on Marino. Out of the corner of my eye I see Alessandra's limp body spin helplessly, whip marks dripping blood.

How long did this go on? I was only gone for two hours.

How could he do this much damage?

He steps close enough that I can see the red veins in the whites of his eyes. "I could have you strung up next to her in a matter of minutes for insubordination."

I bare my teeth. "Try it."

That earns me a genial smile, the kind he uses on circus guests he despises. The ones who care about safety and practicality instead of the show. "You might be able to take down a few strong men, but not all of them. And they listen to me. Look around."

I take his advice. The people who'd simply been enduring are watching carefully now. I see fear in many of their eyes. Avarice in a few. Though the smart ones are watchful. This is a power struggle, plain and simple. They don't want to be on the wrong side of this. No one does. Not even me, but I don't know how the hell to get out of it.

Emerson looks blank. We've become some-times-friends, but I wouldn't want to test that. I don't want to find out if he'd help string me up.

And Wolfgang? He looks pissed but then that's his usual expression.

He's probably armed with a handful of knives, which he can throw with alarming accuracy from long distances, not to mention that his meaty fists could do damage. It's always been a mystery how that much brute force manages precision.

I'm well and truly outnumbered.

Her dangling body catches my attention. It's a mistake to look up. A mistake to see where the rope has cut into her ankle, because the skin there isn't meant to support her entire body weight. Blood as bright red as the circus tent drips along her shins, upside down.

I should back down, live to fight another day. But I can't.

Can't let it happen.

"Is this what you want?" I ask the performers and the operators alike. "To be beaten like animals? For our pain to be used as entertainment?"

"It's punishment," says a man who has been enjoying the show too damn much. There's even a tent in his fucking pants. "What else is he supposed to do? She endangered the circus."

I don't bother arguing his point about the danger. "I want there to be much stricter safety policies and procedures, but this isn't how we do it."

"Then what?" Wolfgang asks, his voice low. There's genuine curiosity. "If you write a neat little guidebook of your safety rules, and someone breaks it, then what?"

Everyone watches me, some disdainful, some solemn.

They want to know.

"Then they leave the circus. Anyone who endangers the circus has to go." I turn to face Marino with narrowed eyes. This man has been my mentor. Even a father figure. And now he's my enemy. "And right now, Marino is the one endangering the circus."

A gasp ripples through the crowd.

A few murmurs of surprise and speculation.

I never thought of myself as a leader.

I also never thought of myself as a man who would allow a woman to be strung up and whipped bloody against her will, which means I have a choice to make.

"You'll regret this," Marino says, his voice raspy, eyes bright with vicious intent.

"No doubt," I say, ripping the whip from his hold. He's strong, but not strong enough to hold onto it against my hold. "Now get the hell out of the tent."

He takes a step toward me, and I crack the whip.

He stops, because he's a fucking coward. He would use this on a woman, but he's too fucking scared to get hit with it himself even to claim his own circus.

Everyone sees it. Everyone knows.

Whatever respect or fear they had for him dies in that moment.

It's a hostile takeover, not one that happens in boardrooms. It's the animal kingdom. Emerson was right, after all. And I half expect him to kill me for it.

A knife should be lodged in my throat right now.

It's happening. As I watch, in a fluid motion, Wolfgang pulls a knife from his boot. He aims and throws with such casual accuracy it makes crowds of circus-goers gasp. I wait for the pain. The shock to my system. I wait for death.

Instead the knife sails past me.

I even hear the whistle a few inches from my ear.

He missed. How is that possible? Was it an accident? On purpose?

I turn and see the knife slice through the thick rope holding up Alessandra. She crumples into Emerson's arms, who lowers her gingerly to the ground. He looks at me, his expression grim. I turn to see Wolfgang, who gives me a short nod.

This is a coup. And it's happening now.

I crack the whip again. "Cirque des Miroirs belongs to me now. Does anyone disagree?"

Marino is still blubbering threats, but they're useless so long as he won't even come near me. People can see that Emerson and Wolfgang are on my side. That sways them, even if their own loyalty to me wouldn't have.

The workers look wide-eyed, shocked, and… somehow, somehow relieved.

"Do we kill him?" Emerson asks, sounding unconcerned with my answer. It's as casual as anything. *Do we put the tent away? Do we drive to the next town?*

I stare at the man who mentored me, the man who snarls. He won't give up the circus without a fight. If we left him behind, he'd only come after us. How do we stop him?

It digs into a deeper question: how do we punish someone who hurts the circus?

How do we protect ourselves without becoming a monster?

CHAPTER FOUR

Present day

W E SHOULD BE on our way to the next city already, but I gave the order to stop.

I gave the order because I was suspicious.

Because I wanted to find some proof that Sienna was telling the truth.

I walk through empty rows of empty tents. Everyone is already packed up in their RVs, staying dry against the damp. I could find Emerson in his, probably with a woman. Something tugs me toward the big top instead.

The stands have already been put up along with the barricade that draws a circle in the center, the apparatus that the acrobats use packed away.

It's a large empty space except for one man

who stands in the middle.

Whatever he sees on my face doesn't seem to surprise him.

He does a slow clap that echoes in the hollow arena. "I see from the thundercloud above your head that you figured it out, mon ami."

I don't stop walking. I keep going.

He doesn't back away.

He doesn't charge.

He doesn't even lift his hands in defense. There's only acceptance. Even here under the gravity of the moment, there's a twinkle in his eye, mischief.

I'm going to get my answers, but first, I'm going to plow my fist into his face.

I'm going to feel the force sling his body to the ground.

I'm going to hope that there's even an ounce of satisfaction as he crumples.

None. There's none.

And I am left breathing hard, fighting the urge to hit him again and again, unleashing the feral animal inside me.

He opens his jaw wide and then closes it, touching gingerly. "Your right hook is legendary," he says, "I can see why."

"Get up," I tell him.

He reclines on the dirt floor looking as cozy as if it's a plush cushion cropped up on his elbows. He's still wearing his ringmaster's suit. Though he's lost the jacket and the hat somewhere, he's in short sleeves and bespoke pants. "So, you can hit me again? That's not an enticing offer."

"I said get up."

He sighs as if I'm a trial.

But he stands, and then I hit him again. This time, it seems to land harder. Not my actual fist, but the gravity of the situation.

He holds his jaw, panting. "Fuck," he says. "Predictable. That's the problem with this show. I knew what was coming."

I bare my teeth in a cold, humorless smile. "A show, that's all this has been, one that you directed."

He moves slower now, clearly feeling the pain. But he stands up again and spreads his arms. "Well, swing again, my friend, swing again. As many times as it takes to get your anger out, as many times as it takes for you to become Gerard Marino." He looks up. "Or perhaps you would like to string me up by the scaffolding. I'm sure we can find a whip somewhere here, even without the lions and tigers."

A low growl escapes me. "Tell me what the

hell happened. Everything, don't leave anything out."

"Everything," he says faintly, mocking as if it's a complicated story.

"Start talking. Unless you would like to be hit again."

He puts his hands up as if to say, *I'm talking, I'm talking. Don't hit me again.* "Here's the story." Even speaking slightly quieter and more quickly than he normally does, there is still the air of a ringmaster leading me into the show. "Boy meets girl. Girl becomes boy's temporary fortune teller. Boy loses his fucking mind, jeopardizes the whole circus."

"How? Because I already know she climbed up there because she believed that someone was inside, because she was trying to help. That didn't jeopardize the circus."

"It happened long before that," he says, a little anger leashed in his voice. "You were distracted. You didn't care what happened anymore. At times, when you would have been taking care of us, you were busy fucking her."

A disbelieving laugh. "So I'm supposed to live like a monk. Is that it?"

"Oh, you can fuck," he says. "You can fuck women, but you never have. Even when people believed you were with Alessandra, I knew the truth. You have been living like a monk until her."

Images of her flash through my mind. Her body bared to the moonlight. Her expression as she came, reflected in a thousand mirrors in the maze. And all of it, all of those sensual memories overlaid against a backdrop of betrayal. Because what is inherent in each moment that I touched her is trust. Trust that I deserved up until the moment that I didn't.

And now I won't get to touch her again.

"Do it. Whatever you're planning on doing. Kill me. Kick me out of the circus."

"Oh, I will," I tell him, my voice grim. "But first, you're going to explain yourself."

He sighs looking away. "Do you remember that night?"

"The night I took over the circus? Yes, I remember every detail."

"Marino told you you'd live to regret it."

"No doubt I will," I say, echoing the long-ago words.

"The circus is more than a job. It is more than a mistress. It's a wife. It's a lifestyle. It's a god. We need monks to run it. You can fuck around with any woman you meet in town or even inside the circus, you can have your pick of them. But when you choose one, when you want one over anything, over the circus, then the whole thing falls apart. There's a reason why Marino worked for so long."

"He worked because everyone was fucking afraid of him."

"No. He worked because he made the circus his life, and most people aren't willing to do that. Even when they perform and travel, they still want their families, they still want a few moments to themselves each night. And you never did."

"You don't want a person," I tell him, "You want a martyr."

"Yes," he snaps. "What did you think you were being when you stood in front of all of these people here beneath the tent, when you took the whip away from him and snapped it? You became our martyr. And then one day, because you saw some nice pussy, you decided that was over."

Some of the fight drains out of me. I am still furious. I'm still disillusioned. I'd love to blame blindly. But in a twisted way, I can understand it. I did become a martyr that night, even if that isn't what I meant to do. And I have lived and breathed the circus every day and every night since then.

Sienna changed that in a beautiful way.

She made me come alive.

And for that crime, the circus made her pay.

If the circus is a god, it's a vengeful one, a possessive one.

"She was hurting the circus," Emerson says. "Maybe not that night, but every night before. And isn't that what you said? That's what happens. They leave."

Marino would laugh if he could see me now.

He can't see me, of course. He's living in semi-captivity at our farm in Nebraska. That's where I kept him after I ejected him from the circus. I built that farm—where the animals could live out the remainder of their lives in cages. And what is Gerard Marino but a wild animal who performed for the circus? He has his own comfortable cage.

I throw one last punch.

Emerson's not expecting it, so he staggers back before crumpling to the ground in an ungraceful heap.

I stand over him. "I don't know what would've happened had you not interfered. Maybe I would have fallen in love and made babies and settled down in some suburban house with a white picket fence and a dog. Eventually, that might have happened. But now, I'm going to find her. I'm going to stall the entire fucking circus until I find her and beg for her back, and then she will hold the fate of every act of every person in this show in her hands. You were afraid of her power before, know that it's even stronger now."

Then I stalk out of the tent, determined to drive into town to find her.

I'm already taking out my cellphone to call her.

She probably won't answer, but I have to at least try. She can't have gone that far. It's been a few hours, but she didn't have a car or a plane ticket.

She just had money and a small dog.

The memory of the dog pulls me up short. And for a second, I can imagine that suburban house with a picket fence and that little tan dog with one ear up and one ear down. I can imagine Sienna laughing as I come home to her. Imagine her round with my child.

The vision is breathtaking and all the more painful because it was within reach.

As if I conjured him from memory alone, the little dog comes into view, panting from its run, both ears flopping around. Hope rises in my chest. Did she come back somehow against the odds, despite the callous way I sent her away?

Even if it's as simple as forgetting something in my RV, at least I'll have a chance, a chance to speak to her. I look behind the dog as he arrives at my feet.

He goes up on his hind legs, one tiny paw against my shin as if asking for something.

"Where is she, boy?"

He doesn't look back, to indicate that someone is walking behind him. Instead he turns and starts retracing his steps. I start following him, his path, and he trots along beside me as if this is the right thing to do.

Did something happen to her?

Christ, maybe she tripped. Maybe she fell down, the ground is so uneven ever since the rain. Or worse, maybe a scorpion bit her. The hard thing about traveling is that you don't know what the locals know about precautions against wildlife that are dangerous up here.

We learned them over time and share that wisdom, but she didn't know.

Whatever happened, I'll help her.

Everything will be all right. That's what I tell myself.

But as I get further away from the fairgrounds, the little dog trotting a couple feet ahead of me as if to guide me, my weariness rises and rises.

"Where are you taking me?" I mutter. "This better not be a wild goose chase."

The dog just keeps trotting along.

Only when we arrive at our destination, Sienna isn't there.

She hasn't fallen or gotten bit by a scorpion, at least as far as I know.

She's gone.

Vanished.

A flash of silver in the mud reveals her phone.

I crouch down to pick it up. It looks largely unharmed, just covered in mud. I stand up and look around. She's nowhere to be seen. She wouldn't leave her phone behind, at least not willingly.

The dog whines and looks at me imploringly.

Dread sinks in my gut.

Something happened to her, something worse than a scorpion.

She was taken.

And I have a dark suspicion that I know who did it, that it was those bullies I met the same night I met Sienna. Kyle and his two assholes, as she called them.

They were obsessed with her, they wanted her.

But they wanted to possess her as an object, not as a woman.

Did they follow the circus?

Did they lie and wait until she was separated from the pack?

That's what predators do, and I made their job too fucking easy when I sent her away.

CHAPTER FIVE

Sienna

A GIRL HAS a lot of time to think in a trunk.

I think about my father, who was no longer alive. He'd been the monster beside my bed for so long that it felt strange to have him gone. Then again, his absence doesn't seem to matter to my general state of well-being.

He's still dragging me home to Forrester from beyond the grave.

I think about Travis, who managed to escape his bullies and find refuge. He belongs at the circus. He's a clown. A damn good one.

I'm glad one of us got away.

Maybe that's all the hungry rage of a dark small town is willing to lose: one at a time.

I very carefully don't think about Logan. I

don't think about whether he'll miss me. Or whether he feels guilty. Even though he probably does. Not because he cares about me specifically but because he'd save the whole world if he could.

Instead he saves his own world. Cirque des Miroirs.

They belong to him in a way I never did.

The car swerves to the right, sending me into the left side, slamming my legs against hot metal. Fuck. All three men drove Ford trucks to prove their manhood.

The Cadillac I'm in was a concession to their kidnapping plans. Hard to hide a flailing, fighting body in the open bed of a pickup. Not that I could fight very well with both hands tied behind my back.

A bump in the road catapults me into the air. And slams me into the roof of the trunk.

Metal on bruised flesh. I'm battered, suffocating in the hot air, but I won't make a sound. Not a moan. Not a plea. I made all the sounds before they stuffed me in here.

Swearing. Baseless threats. An animalistic howl of defeat.

The car stops with a hard screech, and I roll into the hard front of the trunk.

Car doors slam.

The trunk opens.

Sunlight blinds me. Dry West Texas air feels almost cool and breezy after being baked for hours in a tin can.

"Bathroom break." Kyle sounds curt. "Don't make a fuss or someone will get hurt."

"Fuck you," I say hoarsely.

"Someone inside the place will get hurt," he amends.

A hand on my arm hauls me out of the car. My legs feel like jelly, and against my will, I slump against him. He embraces me which is crueler than letting me fall to the ground.

"Shhh," he mutters, running soothing hands up and down my back. "This will be over soon."

"I wish," I say between gritted teeth.

I take a staggering step away from him and almost fall down again. Apparently a long bumpy ride in the desert can turn my legs into jelly.

The gas station looks like it's been closed for a decade. Paint peeling off the wooden sign, the entrance to an ancient car wash grinning with blue rubber teeth.

A flickering Marlboro sign is the only proof that it's open.

That's probably why the boys almost passed it. And probably why they swerved to stop here.

Not many people around to hear me scream.

Faded posters advertising alcohol and tobacco wallpapered the windows. Inside a young man sat behind bulletproof glass, reading on his phone.

"Where's the restroom?"

The attendant doesn't look up, just grunts and gestures vaguely toward the other side of the store.

I try to will him to look up, to notice the way Kyle is holding my arm so tight the skin around it is turning white.

Help me. Please.

I imagine yelling the words. Would he believe me? Would he call the cops? Or would Kyle and the Assholes find a way to harm him, even through the bulletproof glass?

"Give them the key," he says without looking up.

A little girl appears from behind the counter, pushing open the divider that was clearly unlocked. So much for safety behind the glass. She has tight braids and a suspicious frown. I give her a forced smile so she doesn't question me. I don't want them noticing there's a problem now that there's a kid involved.

"You 'spanic?" she asks.

I've been asked this plenty of times, especially

in Texas. Something about the blend of Asian and white heritage.

"She's Indonesian," Kyle says, his voice tempered with pride and gentle encouragement. As if he likes kids. As if he likes *me*, which turns this entire thing into a farce.

How does someone evil look kind?

The guy behind the counter doesn't even look up from his phone to check on his daughter.

I'm not even sure he would if Kyle looked less wholesome, but still. It's a mind fuck.

Kyle half-drags me toward the bathroom and pushes me inside. There's a flimsy lock with the copper plating rusting away. It wouldn't keep him out for very long. There are bars on the small bathroom window, which makes this entire gas station seem even more sketchy. Who's breaking into the bathroom?

No magical escape routes in here.

Nothing to do except actually use the toilet…

And pray I don't catch something.

Then again, that would serve Kyle right. I know what he plans for me. He wants me to be a good little wife.

I wash my hands in a sink that's probably teeming with bacteria. My reflection in the rusty metal mirror looks even worse than I feel, which is saying something. There's a gash on my chin and dried blood on my face. My cheek is bruised. My eyes are bloodshot.

I don't look scared.

I'm too exhausted for that.

Too weak to fight back, to do anything but give in and let go.

I look defeated. This is how Kyle sees me.

But it's not how I feel deep inside.

It's how he sees me, though, which is an advantage. A small one. I'll have to make it work for me.

I want to break the mirror, to feel the glass cut me and taste my own blood, but I can't risk the noise.

A rap on the window.

I look up, expecting to see a bird tapping its beak.

Instead there's a child, her face pressed to the filthy glass.

I manage to hold in my scream. Barely.

It's the girl from inside the station. She points to the metal handle. It's the kind of window where you turn it to open a few inches. I might have been able to push the dog through, if he were still with me. Maybe. There's no way a person is going through.

Though even if I could get out I'd have hundreds of miles of unforgiving desert and dangerous wildlife to contend with.

"Hi," I say, my voice strained from hours locked away in stifling heat.

"Where's Indonesian?"

I don't have time for a geography lesson. Then again, maybe that's all I have left: time. Time before Kyle arrives back in Forrester. Time before he touches me.

Time before he breaks me.

"Indonesia? It's far away," I say. "The other side of the world."

"How do you get there?"

"By plane, I assume. I wouldn't know."

"You've never been there?"

I've only seen photos online. Photos of beautiful scenery and architecture. Photos that I'd felt exactly zero emotional connection to. "No."

"Then how are you from there?"

"My mom is from there."

"I don't have a mom."

It hit me in the chest. Fuck. "I'm sorry."

"Do you need help?"

"No."

"That means yes."

"How does that mean yes?"

"People who don't need help look confused and ask me why I would think that. You got this weird look on your face like you have to poop and then lied."

Little lie detector. In that case I'd better go with the truth. "It's better if you don't get involved."

"I can call someone. After you leave, I can call someone."

Hope beats in my chest. The offer is too good to pass up. Once we're gone they'll be safe. "Yes. Please."

"Who should I call?"

That's a good question. There's my mother. I can't imagine her doing anything but freaking the hell out. There's Maisie, who would be more resourceful… but how could she fight Kyle and the Assholes? It would only get her hurt.

Logan Whitmere, my mind supplies.

My mind is an idiot.

Logan Whitmere kicked me out. Would he come and rescue me if I called him? Maybe. Only out of a sense of duty. He doesn't actually care about me. He doesn't trust me, which hurts more than anything.

For all I know, he would assume it was another stunt.

Like the fucking Ferris wheel.

For as long as I live I will never go on another Ferris wheel. Not even if it's a beautiful sunny day.

"B. Jones," I say. "Brian Jones. He's a State Trooper. Call 911 and get them to find Brian Jones. Tell them the girl from the circus is in trouble."

The girl from the circus might be Alessandra. Or Cat. It might be a lot of people.

"The one with the black eye."

She snorts. "So you had a black eye, but you don't need help. Right."

Snarky little brat. I can't help but smile. She reminds me of myself. "Thank you for this."

An eye roll. "Whatever."

She disappears with barely a sound as her feet drop to the hard-packed earth outside. A bang on the door startles me, and I whirl around, facing the metal door with its ancient maintenance log. Faded ink on yellow paper proclaims this was last serviced two years ago. Lovely.

"Let's go, sweetheart," Kyle calls through the door, his voice gruff. No one would know he wasn't an impatient boyfriend.

The word *sweetheart* runs through my veins like acid.

I don't want to be anyone's sweetheart.

I want to be called *Sunset*.

I want to be Logan's sunset.

Then again, sunsets are always on their way out the door. Maybe that's why he called me that. Because he always knew he'd say goodbye.

CHAPTER SIX

Logan

T FEELS LIKE leaving a part of my body behind. Something nonessential like a limb. A leg. I'm still alive, but I'll never be quite the same after Emerson's betrayal. There was a time I didn't trust him not to kill me. Then he backed me that fateful night. Trust grew and grew.

I would have counted him as my best friend, alongside Wolfgang.

Now he's no longer in the circus.

I'm on the way toward another body part. My heart.

The entire circus is headed back to Texas but it will take many days for them to make the trek. I'll be taking the faster way of a flight into a small airport and then an SUV rental. Wolfgang is in the passenger seat. Travis is in the back, my personal resource to the small town of Forrester where Sienna was born and raised.

Where she's most likely being held against her will.

My knuckles turn white on the steering wheel. *Hold on, Sienna. I'll find you.*

Wolfgang breaks the silence. "She'll make it through this."

I swallow hard. She survived so much already.

She shouldn't have to survive more.

A faded sign says *Welcome to Forrester,* an old-fashioned painting of a mural with a scenic lake with tall trees and a few birds flying away. Beautiful. Picturesque. And entirely a façade. As much of a show as the acrobats and music in the circus.

The serene landscape hides a dark underbelly.

Prejudice. Cruelty. This town never accepted Sienna Cole for being different.

They also refuse to let her go.

"Tell us what we're walking into," Wolfgang demands.

Travis fidgets. He's been in pain ever since hearing that Sienna was taken, white-faced, tight-lipped. Willing to help, which is why he's here. "Kyle was her friend. He was... my friend, too.

The three of us would spend time in the lake by his house. His mom was nice to us. Always made us grilled cheese sandwiches, let us have soda, that kind of thing."

"What went wrong?"

He gives an uneven shrug as I watch through the rearview mirror. "I started to show. I couldn't… hide who I was. That I'm different than the other guys. That I'm gay. Kyle's dad had never been a fan of us, but he put his foot down when he found out."

"What about Sienna?" My voice is filled with gravel.

"We were all developing, you know. Growing up. I think he wanted her that way, and she said no. So he spread the rumor that she was loose."

A low growl escapes me.

"It really backfired on him because after that every guy wouldn't leave her alone. Kyle was never able to get over her, and she wouldn't give him the time of day. It pissed him off, so they would pick on me, bully me, because they knew she would come to my rescue." He makes a pained sound. "I tried to push her away, so she wouldn't get hurt, but it never worked."

Leather creaks beneath my hold. "She was fucking alone."

"And maybe I hated her because she was like me. Because she was an outcast like me, but she was still so fucking strong all the time. She could laugh in their faces. I could never do that."

Wolfgang clears his throat. "Where does Kyle live?"

"On the west side of town. A big house. His father came from a long line of ranchers, but he sold the land. Now he sells insurance, but he doesn't need to work at all. His real job is coaching Kyle in football and pretending to run Forrester with his buddies."

"I can't wait to meet him," I say with complete honesty.

"Wait," Wolfgang says, his voice low.

"This bastard—"

"You think I don't know? We don't need this guy and his small town, small-minded cronies alerting the authorities before we find her and have her safe."

"Fuck."

Travis pipes up. "He plays poker with the sheriff every week."

It doesn't end up mattering.

When we roll to a stop on the expensive cobblestone-paved driveway, an older woman comes out, worry in her eyes. "Kyle? Are you here about

Kyle?"

We step out of the vehicle.

"Travis," she says, her eyes lighting up as she sees the third passenger in the truck. "Look at you all grown up." He seems bashful in front of the older lady.

"Hello, Mrs. Moore. It's good to see you."

Her eyes dim. "I'm sorry you stopped coming around." She hesitates. "I'm sorry, you weren't welcome here anymore. I tried to tell them. They were wrong. But they just…"

"It's okay," he says. "I understand."

She looks fierce. "You shouldn't have to understand. You should have been safe here in this house, in this town. You shouldn't have had to leave to go to the circus with those…" Her gaze flicks to us, a little fearful, a little wary. We're used to that kind of look, but it's especially offensive when it comes from someone who ran this kid out of town. At the very least, her family did.

"I'm his brother," I tell her.

Her eyes widen. "Oh." Realization works through her head as she understands the connection that Travis's mother was knocked up by someone who worked for the circus. Someone like me. Judgment flashes through her eyes, then it's replaced by sorrow. She shakes her head. "The world is so crazy sometimes," she says.

"I like the circus," Travis says. "I like being a clown. It's fun to put on a costume and pretend to be someone else, to make people laugh instead of making them angry."

She sighs, "I don't suppose you're here because you have good news about Kyle, are you?"

"Where is your son, Mrs. Moore?" Wolfgang steps forward, looking severe. She turns to him and all the pretenses drop. The judgment, the wariness. There's only a sad mother left standing defeated in front of a beautiful house.

"I don't know where he is. He's been missing for weeks. I keep hoping. I kept thinking maybe, but no." She shakes her head. "He's gotten into some trouble, hasn't he? That's why you're here looking for him?"

"I believe he took Sienna Cole away from the circus, that he's keeping her against her will." Shock passes through her, and then she suddenly looks 10 years older. She looks ancient. A mother who has prayed and prayed and prayed. It was never enough. Whether she could have done something to prevent this or not, it doesn't matter. The fact is, she doesn't know where her son is. I believe that much to be true. I can see the genuine fear in her eyes. Fear that we're right, fear that we'll find him. Fear that we will kill him. She should be afraid.

"Thank you for your time, Mrs. Moore," Wolfgang says. We turn to get back in the truck.

"Wait," she wrings her hands together. "I don't know what he's done or where he is, but you have to understand, he loves her."

"No," I say, shaking my head. "That's not love. It's obsession." I get into the car without another word. I don't tell her that I understand Kyle far more than I would like to. I don't tell her that I know how it feels to want to hold onto Sienna so tight it leaves bruises on her beautiful skin. That I want to keep her against all reason, all logic. That I would do anything to have her, possess her. I don't tell her that her son and I are the same.

CHAPTER SEVEN

Sienna

THIS ISN'T WHERE I expected to end up when we pulled up in the back of a truck. The skills that made me a good a good tarot card reader, the hypervigilance, are back. And they're telling me to play a long, to put on a good show, that I'm in more trouble now than I was in the trunk of the car. Because the mastermind behind all this is more than a few violent, horny men.

I'm getting my first tarot reading.

Oh, I've given plenty of them, making up bullshit based on what the internet taught me about tarot cards and what I could read of people. That old hypervigilance from years of abuse helped me do a decent portrayal, but it was always an act.

What's happening now is not an act.

At least, not in this woman's mind.

She smiles at me, gorgeous even in her advancing years. Beautiful smile. Beautiful hair. Only her eyes reveal her wildness. I wonder if they helped people believe that she had a connection to the mystical world, back when she was the fortune teller for Cirque des Miroirs.

"Let's see what the spirits have to say," she says, shuffling the cards.

"I wish I could participate," I say, my teeth ground together. "Unfortunately my hands are tied. Literally."

Another brilliant smile. "Your participation is not required. The cards do all the work."

"Considering I've been a fortune teller for a few weeks now, I beg to differ." I shift, trying to assuage the ache in my arms. The angle they're bent back isn't extreme, but not being able to stretch them out has made them scream in pain. I long to reach up.

The fact that I would undoubtedly do violence to the woman in front of me is just icing on the cake. Unfortunately, she knows that. Probably the cards told her the super insightful tidbit that kidnapping someone doesn't exactly make them friendly.

"You were a fake," she says, her voice flat. "You stole what was mine."

"You left."

"I was going to come back," she says, her eyes wilder now. It isn't mysticism making them that way. It's insanity. "I always come back. Logan knows that."

"I guess he didn't know," I say, taunting. "Or maybe he didn't care if you came back."

Maybe it's not a good idea to taunt your captor, but I've given up on being the good girl a long time ago. People are going to judge me, they're going to fuck with me, so I might as well fight back. Even if it's only with words.

She flips a card over, revealing an image of a tall building.

A tall building that's on fire.

Lovely.

"Destruction," she says, a gleeful glint in her dark eyes. How can she look so much like Cat but also so evil? Then again Cat did lie to Logan about me. She's just better at hiding it. "Chaos. This represents your past. Your childhood."

"It's Forrester," I say, feeling almost thoughtful despite the rope tied around my wrists. Forrester is on fire, though not in a literal sense. It burns through its own people. It leaves them empty husks, brittle and dark-edged.

She nods, almost pleased. She might be tutoring me on tarot readings for how approving she looks for a moment. Her hand makes a wide, sweeping gesture as she pulls the second card.

Three swords pierce a heart.

"A little dramatic," I say, my voice dry even as my heart pounds.

"Heartbreak," she says, the corner of her lip curled up. "You've experienced that, haven't you? A recent little sorrow. A small bit of grief."

Recent. Small. Is that how I would describe what happened with Logan?

It's how I *should* describe it.

We were nothing. Less than nothing. Not even dating in any official capacity. No future possible between a successful circus owner and his transient fortune teller.

The way it ended… sucked.

It really sucked.

Confirmation that he was just like everyone else.

Well, I could get over it trapped in this dusty cabin as easily as anywhere else.

She pulls the final card. A man is suspended upside down. The Hanged Man.

"The ultimate card of surrender," she says,

sounding pleased with herself. Too pleased. It can't mean anything good. "You'll be a sacrifice to the greater good."

"Exactly which greater good is that?"

"The good of the circus, of course."

My throat feels dry, though whether it's the revelation or the lack of water recently, I couldn't say. "That's convenient for you."

"Yes," she says, beaming.

"Then again, maybe I'll be the one to choose the sacrifice. Maybe I'll be the one to get rid of you. Logan might even give me a medal. Does the circus have medals? Like the Barnum & Bailey Medal of Honor? The Ringling Brothers Purple Heart?"

"Blasphemy," she growls.

Her semi-religious fervor for Cirque des Miroirs became apparent as soon as I met her. Kyle and the Assholes dumped me up here and tied me to an iron-framed bed, where I'd finally fallen into a reluctant, dreamless sleep. It wasn't precisely relaxing, but my body needed rest if I had a chance of escaping.

When I woke up, she was watching me, humming an off-tune circus melody.

Creepy as fuck.

"Madame Galilea sees the stars," I say in my

fake performer's voice, more whispery and mysterious than hers. "And the stars know what has been and what will be."

"You're a fake."

"Precisely. Which is how I know how easy it is to make the cards say whatever you want. Especially when you have a stacked deck."

Her eyes narrow. "I don't cheat."

The irony of this woman claiming not to cheat, when her entire career has been based on fleecing strangers in every city. Not to mention her little extracurricular activities tricking men into motel rooms and then stealing from them.

Some people like to accuse others of their own activities.

It's an irony I've never fully understood but one I've learned to accept.

The person who calls me names also calls me a bully.

The cheerleader who sleeps around also calls me a whore.

And the man who promised me a safe space? Well, he called me a liar.

My heart squeezes.

There's no point defending myself. It doesn't work. No point arguing with people who are blind with their own ironic self-righteousness. "Is this little show over?" I ask, my voice flat. "I would pay you for the reading, but I'm afraid I lost my wallet somewhere in the desert."

"You may be smug," she tells me. "But we both know that I've been protecting you from the worst that Kyle Moore has to offer. He wants to marry you. He believes it, and I may have given him a reading or two to convince him it will come to pass."

"Asshole," I say with a very fake cough.

"What is going to happen when he decides he's waited long enough?"

I have no retort to that, not with the dread rising in my chest. She cackles as she drags me back toward the iron bedframe. It would be a reasonable time to fight if my hands weren't tied behind my back. If my ankles weren't tied together. If she didn't have a gun hidden in the folds of her gown, the same gun she used to subdue grown-ass men.

"Why are you doing this?" I ask her before she leaves.

She turns back to look at me. Her eyes, rather than glee, show a form of sympathy. The kind you'd use for a rabbit in your snare, right before you took it home and cooked it. "You and I are much alike."

I snort. "You don't even know me."

"You are misunderstood, though not by accident. They wish to misunderstand you. It's easier to make you the villain in their story than to realize that they are the problem."

"Based on what?"

"The town slut. The troublemaker."

A shiver runs through me. "Kyle talks a lot of shit."

"Logan told me he'd met someone. I investigated, of course. I'm protective of him. And the circus. Found out it was a little hussy, but here's what you must understand, I don't judge you. All women are thrown onto the stakes. They don't need fire to burn us alive."

"If you don't judge me, why the…?" I shake the bed, which rattles ominously. "Why the whole kidnapping and murder thing?"

"I was prepared to let Logan have his little fling. Men need sex. They need domination. He could have you… as a treat. Then I heard that he offered you a job. My job. And I knew that I had to remove you from the picture completely."

"Ah, so classic greed. You dressed it up in the occult, but it's baser than that."

"What do you think the tarot cards read, my child? They read lust and sinister intentions. They reflect the darkness in humanity. That's why people love them. That's why they pay me money to tell them they're bound for destruction." She leaves me with those parting words.

Then I'm left alone to stare up at the dust motes dancing in the sunlight.

Funny, how they don't seem to care whether they swim through the air for a joyful family scene or a lonely captive tragedy. Funny, how the world just keeps turning even when I'm trapped. But then it's not really new. I opened Pandora's box years ago, simply by existing. By being a girl and being weak and being afraid. I've been dealing with the demons ever since. Maybe the Hanged Man card has a point. It's time to surrender to my fate.

CHAPTER EIGHT

Logan

THE SUV ROLLS to a stop in front of a modest yellow house, overgrown weeds lining the front walkway. Sienna's house. It looks sad despite its general upkeep. The dainty white flowers planted along the front only highlight the sorrow cloaking the place.

Wolfgang squeezes my shoulder before we climb out of the truck.

My heart pounds as I raise my fist and knock.

The door creaks open, and Banyu Cole's fearful eyes peer up. "Who are you?"

I take a deep breath, meeting her gaze. "I'm Logan Whitmere. Owner of Cirque des Miroirs. Your daughter's…" Lover. Betrayer. "Boss. We need to talk."

"Sienna? Is she okay?" Banyu hesitates, glancing between me and Wolfgang. She swallows hard before stepping aside. "You must come in."

We follow her into the dimly lit living room, the air heavy with tension. Banyu perches on the edge of an armchair, wringing her hands in her lap.

I stand, unable to sit on the stained armchair where her bastard of a father once sat. "Have you heard from Sienna recently?"

Her face falls. "Then it's true. She's missing."

"I'm sorry."

She shakes her head, expression pinched. "The last time I talked to her on the phone she was in Arizona. There was some story about a scorpion."

Everyone had freaked out, which is ridiculous. Sienna had been unafraid of the lethal little arachnid. She would have taken a baseball bat to it if I hadn't stepped in to handle it for her. The memory makes my chest tighten. She was protecting the circus. Why didn't I see that?

I lean forward, pulse racing. "Do you have any idea who might have taken her?"

"I don't know." Banyu's voice wavers. "She's friends with Maisie Young. She lives a few miles from here with her family. She's doing correspondence classes for college online. That is what

I wanted Sienna to do, but we don't have a computer. And her father…"

Her father. I wish I could kill him again.

"We heard your husband passed away," Wolfgang says gently. "Our condolences."

Banyu's eyes flick to Wolfgang, then back to me, gaze shifting away. "Thank you."

I swallow against the lump in my throat and reach for Banyu's hand. She startles at my touch before relaxing into it.

"Can you think of anything else?" I ask, giving her hand a gentle squeeze. "Anything you can tell us could help. Anyone who didn't like her."

Banyu's eyes shimmer with tears as she meets my gaze. "A lot of people in town didn't like her. They don't like me, either. Because we're different. And because it's easier to pretend they did not see our bruises if they could also say they hated us."

She trails off with a helpless shrug.

She looks like Sienna but also different. Older, of course. More tired. More exhausted. It's a stark contrast to Sienna's vitality. They have the same features but an entirely different energy. At least, they did. What will happen to Sienna's beautiful strength after this? Even if I find her alive, will she have the same spirit? I want to believe that nothing could tear her down, but that's a futile hope. It's ignorance, not knowing how harsh the world could be.

The woman on the floral couch in front of me knows all about the harshness.

She looks worried about Sienna but also resigned.

She's been worried about her daughter for a long time without doing much. I don't say that to blame her. Sometimes survival is all a person can manage.

Anger burns in my stomach. "Do you know someone named Kyle Moore?"

Dark eyes widen. "They were friends. As children. Even before she became close with Maisie. Travis, Kyle, and Sienna. They used to swim at the lake together and catch frogs. They'd climb trees together. They built a treehouse together."

It's hard to imagine a worm like Kyle being friends with Sienna. Or hell, even Travis. I remember Mrs. Moore's reaction to Travis, so warm and loving...and sad. "What changed?"

She closes her eyes, revealing fragile, blue-veined eyelids. "Forrester happened. He grew up enough to see that we were hated. Because we are different. Because we are dangerous. They hate

Sienna because of the shape of her eyes. They hate Travis because of who he is."

"Names," I say, my voice hard.

She offers me a soft, almost musical laugh. It reminds me so much of Sienna that my heart aches. "It would simply be a census report of who lives in Forrester. It's everyone."

How can it be everyone? But I know. It's the reason people join the circus. To escape. It's the reason Sienna came to me. I knew her father was abusive. That was why I drove her that night. I hadn't stepped foot inside the house, though. I hadn't seen the chipped wooden furniture carefully polished or the heavy drapes keeping out every ounce of sunlight. I hadn't been able to imagine the prison she'd grown up inside.

Hell, if she wanted to climb the Ferris wheel in a storm, I should have been there with a fucking ladder. Why shouldn't she get to live her life, finally?

Why shouldn't she get to own her choices after being voiceless for so long?

"Anything else you can think of?" I ask, my voice hoarse.

Banyu's brows furrow. "She worked at the Coffee Bean. She said Bart Reinhard would ask her out sometimes, that she kept telling him no."

Another bastard to interrogate. "Thank you. You've given us a place to start."

A flicker of hope sparks in Banyu's eyes. "You really think you'll find her?"

"We have to try." I pull her into a hug and she relaxes into my embrace. "Thank you. For everything."

Banyu nods against my chest before pulling away. A determined set to her jaw, the fear in her eyes replaced by steely resolve.

"Find her," she says softly. "Bring her home."

I share a look with Wolfgang, determination etched into the lines of his face. We don't have any more information than when we started, except for seeing that Sienna was fighting for her goddamn life in this backward town.

"We will," I promise Banyu, voice firm with conviction.

She offers a sad smile, eyes glistening once more. "Be careful. Sienna has been through so much already. She's strong, but..." Banyu hesitates, gaze drifting toward the window as if she can see beyond the limits of Forrester. "There are still shadows lurking inside. Dark places that haven't yet healed."

I swallow against the lump forming in my throat, chest aching at the thought of Sienna's pain. The scars that mark her heart as much as her skin.

"I know," I whisper. "But she's not alone anymore. I'm going to help her face those shadows, and together we're going to find the light."

Banyu blinks back tears, fragile hope etched into the lines of her careworn face. "You really love her, don't you?"

"With everything I am." The words come without thought, whispered on a breath that trembles with emotion.

Banyu's lips curve into a watery smile. She brushes a kiss against my cheek, eyes shining with gratitude. "Then there is hope. As long as you're by her side, the dark cannot win."

I pull Banyu close once more, heart overflowing. There are no words to express my gratitude, the surge of fierce protectiveness that swells within.

Sienna is my light, my heart, my everything.

And I will stop at nothing to bring her home.

Wolfgang clears his throat, gaze averted to hide the sheen of moisture in his eyes. He's silent for a long moment, jaw working around unspoken words.

When he finally speaks, his voice is rough

with emotion. "We should get going. The trail is already cold, and there are not too many hours of daylight left to waste."

He's right, of course. Every second we delay is another opportunity for Kyle to slip further from our grasp. Or this Bart motherfucker.

I release Banyu with reluctance, features tightening at the thought of what's to come. The hunt. The confrontation. Risking everything to save the woman I love.

"Find her," Banyu whispers, clutching my hands like a lifeline. Like she's afraid to let go. "Please. Promise me you'll bring her home."

I squeeze her hands in silent reassurance, meeting Wolfgang's gaze over her shoulder. My friend offers a sharp nod, jaw set in grim determination.

"We will," I vow, pulse quickening as I straighten away from Banyu's embrace. The time for parting has come, and though my heart aches to leave Sienna's mother behind, I know there's no other choice. Not if I want to keep my promise.

Not if I want Sienna back in my arms where she belongs.

Her home isn't this stifling prison.

It isn't Forrester.

She belongs with the circus.

Banyu's eyes look almost glazed as she studies a wooden china cabinet with glass walls. It matches the rest of the house—trying hard for elegance, desperate fingers clenched on the cliff of civility. "I always thought she was like one of my dolls. They were the only things that were mine, you know. The only thing that Patrick allowed me to have. As if I were a young girl."

"He's gone now," Wolfgang says gently.

Something he knows well because he was there when I killed the man.

I swallow around a knot. "Did Sienna like them?"

"I never let her play with them. She was too much like them already, pretty and trapped. Seeing her touch them would feel like I was keeping her prisoner." Tears spring to her dark eyes. "It didn't matter, though. I should have helped her leave. I should have left with her."

I pause on the threshold, chest tight with emotion. This could be the last time I see her, the last glimpse of the woman who gave Sienna life.

Somehow I know with bone-deep certainty that everything is about to change.

And when we next meet, the future will have shifted into something unrecognizable. A world remade by loss and sacrifice. By the threads that bind us together.

I take a deep breath, steeling my nerves.

And step into the sunlight.

The door creaks shut behind us, a hollow ache blooming in my chest.

Silence follows, heavy and oppressive, until Wolfgang clears his throat. "Now what?"

Frustration simmers in my veins, a bitter poison I struggle to contain. "We keep looking," I say, my voice preternaturally calm, fists clenching at my sides as I look toward Travis and Wolfgang. "We tear this shithole town apart if we have to, but we're not leaving until we find her."

Wolfgang sighs, scrubbing a hand over the stubble lining his jaw. "And if she's not here? If this was all some wild goose chase? They might have taken her to Vegas, for all we know."

I flinch as if struck, a flare of panic igniting behind my ribs. No. I can't accept that. I won't. "Like most animals, he has a lair. We just have to find it."

I drive deeper into town through quiet streets, past old clapboard buildings and rusty pickups lining the road. Somewhere in this town, the answers are waiting.

Somewhere close by, Sienna is counting the

seconds until we find her.

Actually, knowing Sienna, she's not expecting me to come for her.

She'll expect to do this alone, the same way she's done everything in her life.

"We'll visit the coffee shop."

Wolfgang shakes his head, worry creasing the corners of his eyes. "It's worth a try, though even if it is this Bart Reinhard, he wouldn't keep her at the shop. Too much noise."

We park and walk down the street, scrutinizing each building we pass. Most are small businesses—a diner, a mechanic's shop, a laundromat.

Nothing that looks suitable for holding a hostage.

Fuck, the idea of Sienna as a hostage makes my blood rush.

"He might have storage space. Someplace secluded." I scrub a hand over the scruff lining my jaw, ideas spinning through my mind. "We'll start at the shop and work our way in. Search every building if we have to."

CHAPTER NINE

Sienna

M Y HEAD IS pounding. Every inch of my body aches.

Noise below me.

The dust in the cabin makes my nose twitch. A sunset has come and gone. That's not a good sign. I feel like I've heard about the first twenty-four hours being crucial in a missing person's case.

Then again, someone would have to know I'm missing for it to be a case.

Maybe State Trooper Brian Jones is on it.

Maybe not.

Either way, I have to get out of here now. Myself.

There's no waiting to be saved.

I've never been a princess.

I hear footsteps coming up to the cabin.

It's wrong that Kyle looks wholesome and handsome in the dreary space, holding a bag of greasy sandwiches and a six-pack of beer. He should look like a villain, instead of Forrester's golden child. He had the best chance of getting out of town, more than me or Travis, but he never wanted it. He's the hero here. The one everyone loves. They never understood why he was interested in me. Him bullying me? That made sense to them.

"Morning, sweetheart," he says, putting the food down on the table that so recently held the tarot cards. The Hanged Man. That's my future, unless I change it. Unless I harness it. I refuse to die in this cabin.

He gives me that huge smile that made all the girls spread their legs.

I refuse to get fucked in this cabin, either.

If he only wanted to bully me, I wouldn't be here.

Alessandra is crazy, but she's right about that much.

He wants more.

And he's delusional enough to think it'll actually happen.

It would be simpler if he didn't care about

consent, not even a little. The bindings currently biting into my wrists are a sign that he doesn't care a lot. But part of him has held back from holding me down all these years. After that first time with the Assholes, he hasn't let them touch me, either. That means there's some morality inside him, doesn't it?

Even a grain of moral sand.

"Listen," I say, my heart thumping unevenly. "Thanks for the ride and all, but can we just chalk this up to one of your little stunts? We all laugh because it's a big joke."

He sits down on the mattress beside me, making the springs squeak. "We both know I'm serious about this. About us."

My skin ripples with unpleasant awareness. "There is *no* us."

His fingers stroke my arm, and I force myself to stay there and take it. "I know you're scared, because of what happened. Because I let Randall and Lucas touch you."

"Touch." An uneven laugh escapes me. It's getting harder to pretend to be calm. "They did more than touch. So did you, come to think of it. There's a word for it, I think. When a girl says no. When the guys don't listen. When they do it anyway."

He sighs, as if I'm a pain in the ass. As if I'm his little wife complaining that he slept around. I must be appeased with my weaker feminine feelings, even if he has the right to do that. "Things got out of hand that night. I kept them from touching you after that, didn't I?"

"Their grip felt pretty intense when they shoved me into the trunk."

"You know what I mean. I won't let them have sex with you. That's a promise. One I've kept for years now, even though you've never appreciated it."

The way men in Forrester think them *not* raping you is a favor. A little gift.

It makes my stomach turn over.

And more determined than ever to leave.

Part of me didn't care when he dragged me back to Forrester. I was pissed about the whole kidnapping thing, but over the long ride on rough old upholstery I was resigned to coming home. Maybe it was inevitable. Maybe it's fate that I belong here.

Wrong.

The tarot cards proved that much.

I can choose my own fate, even if it's death.

Pretending comes naturally to me. Years of avoiding my father's fists have taught me to hide what I'm really feeling. Anger? Pissed him off. Sadness? Same. Any sort of feeling was a trigger for him, so I can make my face blank. I heard once that someone who'd been tortured overseas had learned to wipe their bodies clean of any responses. It freaked people out when they returned home, the complete lack of emotion. But it wasn't real. The emotion was there. They had just learned to hide it. My upbringing? It was a form of torture. Years and years of it.

Hypervigilance gave me the ability to read people and tell good fortunes.

Being beaten gave me the ability to hide my true reactions.

They're like superpowers.

Terrible, painful, *useful* superpowers.

"Why?" I ask, keeping my voice low. "Why me?"

Kyle's blue eyes soften. "You're beautiful."

"So it's only the way I look?"

He sports an indulgent smile, revealing gleaming white teeth. "Are you digging for compliments, sweetheart? You don't have to do that. I don't mind telling you that you're the smartest girl in town. That's partly why they don't like you, by the way. They know."

How sweet. Vomit. "So you want me to do

your taxes?"

He lets out a snort. "It's that smart mouth. I can't get enough. I can't wait until you give it to me, because I've had so many fantasies. Other girls don't come close."

Gross. "Maybe I could…" *Don't sound too eager.* "Maybe we could try it. A kiss."

Blue eyes go dark. "I want more than that."

"Just to start with. You know I'm nervous."

"Right." His hand is shaking as he runs it through his hair. "I can be patient for you, Sienna. I can do anything for you."

I resist the urge to shudder at the thought of him touching me. The thought of his hands on me, his breath on my body, makes my skin crawl. But I keep my expression neutral and simmer with anger, biding my time until I can find my way out of this cabin and away from his grasp.

Kyle leans in, his breath hot on my neck. I hold my breath and try not to recoil. "You were made for this."

I don't respond, don't even look at him. Instead, I focus on a knot in the wood ceiling above me. At least until he blocks the view.

He's looming over me, inches away from my face. His eyes are closed, his lips pursed, and he's getting closer. I want to recoil but I can't. Because the bed holds me up. And because I need him to believe this is real.

The musky scent of his cologne clashes with the grease of the fast food he brought inside. I feel like I'm suffocating.

I watch as his lips move toward mine. His face is wreathed in shadows, but I can see the sharp angle of his jaw, the square of his chin. He moves in, closer.

He brushes his lips against mine, and his tongue slowly darts out to taste my mouth. Stale beer. Old toothpaste.

Blue eyes go dark. He looks determined, passionate. His lips curl down in a frown. He looks pissed off, like he always is.

"Kiss me back."

I can feel the heat of his body against mine, the hardness of his hand in my hair, tangling. He holds me still.

I fight his touch… not to pull away but to get closer. It's the only direction to go, anyway. It's the direction of freedom.

He's breathing hard, little staccato intakes of breath. The hairs on my neck stand on end.

And I kiss him.

But it's not a real kiss, not the kind that makes your heart flutter and your knees weak. It's a kiss borne out of desperation, a kiss meant to keep up appearances, a kiss that makes me want to gag.

As he pulls back, I can see the triumph in his eyes. He thinks he's won me over, that I've finally given in to him. Little does he know, I'm just biding my time, waiting for the right moment to escape.

I can feel his hand moving down my body, fingers grazing my breast, and I tense up. I can't let him do this. I need to get out of here, now.

Pretend. You can do this.

Except the only way I know how to feign sexual interest is by pretending that he's Logan. It's a twisted form of pretense, one that makes me confused inside. Do I want Logan? Or do I hate him?

Both feelings bubble up, making my reaction to Kyle look realistic.

My body feels languid, warm. Nipples turn hard beneath the tank top.

His gaze turns hot.

He strokes a hand from the base of my neck over my breast, squeezing with alarming gentleness. I force myself to squirm, only a little, as if I like it, as if I can't get enough.

"You're so soft." His voice is a whisper. "I

knew you would be." His head dips, and I can feel his hot breath through the thin fabric. "I want to make you feel good."

A shiver runs through me. I know what he means. I've heard the *good* he has to offer. The things Kyle and his friends do to girls. I've seen the blood on the bathroom floor after they were done with me.

And now he's going to do those things.

If I don't get out of here now, history will repeat itself.

He strokes the hem of my shirt, and his hand dips in slowly, gently cupping my breast. "You're so beautiful."

My body reacts. My nipples are hard, and I can feel my entire body warming.

Logan. Pretend it's Logan.

I can't pretend he's Logan if I'm thinking about that night with Kyle and the Assholes.

I can feel his hand shaking, his skin clammy.

Kyle's hand—so often hard and cruel, now soft and gentle—cups my breast, his palm damp with sweat. His fingers brush over my nipple. I can feel his arousal, pressing against me. I can feel it through his pants and my jean shorts.

I'm wet. My body is betraying me.

It's letting Kyle win.

I try to think of Logan, but all I can focus on is Kyle's hand on my breast. I can feel him squeezing me, too hard, too tight.

I can feel his eyelashes fluttering against my cheek, his breath on my neck. His tongue darts out, exploring the hollow of my neck, tasting my skin.

His erection rubs against my thigh.

I can feel myself opening up to him, to his touch, as if my body is letting him win.

"Yes," he breathes. "Touch me back."

Then it happens.

Finally.

Fucking finally.

He reaches up to undo the bindings, eager to feel my hands on his muscled body.

His beautiful body full of lies.

Why are men so beautiful?

Why do they lie so much?

In this moment, with the pretend arousal merging into real memories, he *is* Logan. He's every man who's ever hurt me. Who's ever made me want kindness.

Violence and lies and evil.

That's what men are.

The ropes fall to the floor, and he reaches out, touching my face. I recoil at his touch, pulling back, as he frowns. "What's wrong?"

"Nothing." I shake my head.

"Is it because of that circus freak?"

My mouth twists into a frown. I don't want to say his name, to even know he exists.

It's Kyle who's with me now, not Logan.

I remember his lies.

And his kisses.

I stare back at Kyle, searching for any hint of last night, any sign of my childhood friend.

His grip loosens on my face, and he brushes a strand of hair off my cheek. "I forgive you."

"Thank you," I manage to say.

"Let me touch you." His voice is raspy, his eyes dark. "I've dreamed about this."

"Me too." In nightmares.

I can feel his erection riding my leg. A wave of nausea hits me. I want to get out of here before that heady combination of arousal and fear creeps in, before it feels easier to become his monster.

I wiggle my hands to get the blood flowing again.

I want to scream, to fight, to run out of the room before he can touch me.

He reaches for me. There's desire in his eyes, a kind of desperate need to feel something. His lips twist up in a smile. "I've been dreaming about the day you would let me have you. When you'd be mine."

He moves closer. His lips touch my own, but his breath is warm on my neck. I can feel him trembling. I can't look at his face.

"Sienna." His voice is a whisper in my ear, and he exhales, his breath hot. "I want to—"

I don't care what he wants.

With soundless, vital effort, I slam my hands down on his neck. He makes a sound of surprise. Then I shove with my entire body—using my hands and feet. I shove his head into the rusty iron headboard with a loud thump.

A groan of metal is the only sound in the cabin.

His body leans on me heavily.

With one final push, he slumps to the ground.

CHAPTER TEN

Logan

THE COFFEE BEAN is dimly lit. I pause at the entrance, waiting for my eyes to adjust. The little bell above the door falls silent as Wolfgang and Travis enter behind me.

A patter of toenails on dark-grout tiles brings up the rear.

The scent of stale coffee grounds permeates the air. The crush of an espresso machine clamors above the chatter of voices. Suspicious eyes follow us as we stride inside. I don't know whether they recognize us from the circus or whether they're just suspicious of strangers in general. Probably both.

It could be improved by local art or a splash of color.

Instead we have yellowed walls with black mold spots. This is where Sienna worked for years, starting part time in high school and then full time for the six months since she graduated. It's where she might have come back to work if she hadn't been taken.

My stomach drops.

This is what I consigned her to.

Fuck me.

The cute little drawing of coffee beans on the chalkboard had been a glimmer of hope in a dim place. It's been clumsily erased, leaving the faintest imprint of a walking, smiling coffee bean behind. Over the top someone has scrawled *Coffee – 50 cents.*

Even for a small-town coffee shop that's cheap.

I'm imagining instant coffee from the grocery store bought in bulk.

The place has definitely been struggling since Sienna left.

The counter is empty, as if she's about to appear from the back room with a new jug of milk. An older woman has an empty cup of coffee in front of her, the dark dregs at the bottom, red lipstick marring the lip. So clearly someone is working today.

A familiar laugh catches my attention and my stomach drops.

Emerson sits in the back, one eye swollen shut, an insouciant grin on his face.

Shock holds me still for one second, two. What the hell is he doing here? He's supposed to be thousands of miles away right now.

He's sitting with a blonde young woman wearing a white-dotted peasant top and ragged jean shorts. I wonder briefly, distantly, who the hell she is.

Not that it matters.

The shock coalesces into rage.

Emerson Durand is a dead man.

He doesn't seem particularly concerned about that, at least on the surface. In fact to those who don't know him, he looks welcoming. Taunting. The dog runs up to him and barks… though with excitement, not anger, the traitorous little shit.

"So the prodigal circus owner returns," he says, reaching down to pet the dog.

My hands curl into fists at my sides. That black eye is my doing, a reminder of the betrayal that led us here. No fear shows on his handsome face, but his foot taps nervously under the table. He's prepared to be beaten to a fucking pulp.

He's prepared to die.

Good.

Wolfgang's hand clamps down on my shoulder, holding me in place. "We don't have time for this," he mutters.

"It'll only take a minute to twist his neck."

"Think of the mess. The authorities."

Fuck. This is not the place to murder a man.

The young woman seated at the table slips pieces of her pastry beneath the table, reminding me that I haven't fed the dog since we last ate. How often are dogs supposed to be fed? I probably need to get dog food at some point. Right now he's having what looks like a slice of pumpkin loaf hand-fed to him.

Emerson waves a hand, without a care in the world. "No need to get your knickers in a twist. I come in peace." His remaining eye gleams with mischief. "In fact, I may have some information that could help with your little rescue mission."

I take a steadying breath and force myself not to kill him. We need all the help we can get, even if it comes from a snake like Emerson. "What is it?"

He leans forward, steepling his fingers. The other patrons have gone back to their conversations, but their gazes continue to flick our way. "It seems our dear Sienna has gotten herself into quite the predicament."

I measure the distance from here to the dimly lit EXIT sign. "I think I could stuff your body in a dumpster back there and be gone before the sheriff even gets up out of his chair."

"Patience, my dear boy." Emerson leans back and gestures to the young woman beside him. "It seems Kyle has been very interested in your lady love. Something that her bestie here… What was your name again? Oh yes, Maisie Young."

Maisie looks very young indeed. And nervous. And slightly turned on.

Emerson has that effect on women.

Sienna's friend. Her mother had thought that, too. It's convenient to find her here. Worry darkens her blue eyes. "Kyle was obsessed with her. He always thought they'd get married."

"Impressive," Emerson says, "considering they never dated."

"He's never been particularly concerned with consent." Maisie's voice cracks.

Red washes across my vision at her words. My hands clench into fists again as a growl rumbles in my chest. No one hurts Sienna. Not anymore.

Not if I have anything to say about it.

"Maisie also has some ideas about where they're keeping her," Emerson says.

"Where?" The word bursts from me in a snarl.

A sly smile stretches across Emerson's face. "Now now, no need to get testy. Aren't you glad I decided to help after all? Come on. Aren't you glad I came along?"

As much as I despise him, we need this information. "Tell me where she is."

Emerson leans back, steepling his fingers once more. "Let's make a deal. I get my job back in exchange for the information I learned. It seems a small price to pay."

I slam my hands on the table, rattling the cups and causing Emerson to jerk back in alarm. "Enough games. Tell me where Sienna is right now or so help me—"

"There's no need for violence." Emerson holds up his hands in a placating gesture, but his eyes have gone hard. "I'm trying to help you, you suspicious bastard."

"We don't need your form of help," Wolfgang growls from beside me.

I take a deep breath, trying to calm my frayed nerves.

Maisie stands up, which is a courageous move in a room full of angry men, violence hovering beneath the surface. "I don't care about your little pissing contest. I only care about Sienna. If she's in trouble, I don't expect the Forrester Police Department to do anything about it. I don't really know or trust you guys either, but you might be all she has."

"I'm going to find her," I promise, my voice hoarse.

Her eyes narrow. "Then what?"

As much as I despise the delay, I'm grateful that Sienna had at least one friend in this godforsaken shithole town. "Then I'm going to win back her trust."

"And if you can't?"

A straight shot to the heart, as piercing as one of Wolfgang's knives. He has them strapped all over his body—in his boot and beneath his leather vest. He might as well have stabbed me, because that's what I deserve.

Sienna shouldn't trust me again.

I failed her.

"Then I'll let her go."

Maisie studies me for a long moment. "He has a hunting cabin. It's Randall's actually, passed down from his uncle. A real primitive place, from what I understand. No plumbing. I don't think they even do actual hunting, except when they're trying to impress Kyle's dad."

"Where is it?"

"She's never been," Emerson says. "But I have a source in city hall. They looked at the deeds with the last name Todd and found a tract of land to the southeast."

"What the fuck kind of source would you have in city hall?" Wolfgang demands.

Emerson grins. "We stayed in this tiny city for days. That's enough for me to fuck my way through the entire female population."

"I already regret trusting you," Maisie says.

"I never trusted him," Wolfgang says.

"Will you keep the dog?" I ask Maisie. "He belongs to Sienna." And I refuse to believe that I won't get her back safely. "Only until we have her back. Otherwise he'll just end up hurt."

"Of course." Her expression clouds. "We have three at home. Sienna loved them but her parents never let her get a dog. I'm glad she finally got one."

For only a few days. "He doesn't have a name yet."

Emerson studies me. "You won't get far without my information. Kyle's not an idiot. He'll stay low. You go out there searching the wilderness, you'll never find her."

"Fuck you." I don't trust him, not after what happened with Sienna. But we're running out of time and options and his information could be our only chance.

"Kyle still lives with his mother, but she hasn't seen him. The Assholes both rent rooms above the hardware shop. Nowhere to keep a body."

A body. Fuck.

I'm coming for you, Sienna. Just hold on a little longer. I'm going to get you out of this. No matter what.

My blood boils at the thought of Sienna in that monster's grasp.

Sienna's face flashes in my mind and determination floods my veins, wiping away any remaining doubt. I'll do whatever it takes to get her back.

Even if that means trusting Emerson, at least for now.

"Take me with you," Emerson says, his voice gone low, and in a rare move for him, sincere. "Let me make this right for you."

My hands unclench as I meet Emerson's gaze. "Fine."

Emerson's sly smile returns. "That's more like it."

"He may not kill you," Wolfgang says. "But I might."

Tears make Maisie's eyes glitter like diamonds. "I knew how hard her life was. But I didn't know how to help her." She picks up the dog who licks a tear off her face. "The cops always sided with Kyle. They didn't care enough to do anything about her father. And now this."

A pang shoots through my chest. So Sienna went through that hell alone, with no one to turn to for help. The thought shreds my heart into pieces.

I give Maisie a hard nod. It's a promise, that nod. "It's not your fault. Sienna is strong. She'll come through this like she did everything else."

Maisie nods. "I'll watch over the dog until you bring Sienna home."

"Stay in town," I tell Travis. "Ask around. Call me if you find out anything."

He nods, looking relieved that he isn't involved in a firefight.

I turn to Wolfgang and Emerson, my friend and my betrayer. "We go in tonight, under cover of darkness. Emerson, you scout the land where we think Kyle is keeping Sienna. Then we launch a surprise attack." My hands curl into fists as I picture wrapping them around Kyle's throat. "No one hurts Sienna and gets away with it."

Wolfgang's lips twist into a grim smile. "Let's teach those bastards a lesson."

Emerson tilts his head, eyes glinting. "This should be entertaining. I do love a good fight." He cracks his knuckles. "Kyle won't know what hit him."

Not precisely true.

I'll make sure he knows exactly who's hurting him.

Every bruise, every bone that breaks.

When he takes his last breath, he'll know why.

An older woman's shrill voice cuts through. "The circus freaks are back."

I whip around to see a wrinkled woman pointing a bony finger at Emerson. "We don't want your kind here," she snarls, her wrinkled lips lifted in disdain. "Stay away from Maisie. She's a nice girl. Not for the likes of you."

Rage bubbles in my chest, fury clouding my vision. I take a threatening step toward the woman but a firm hand on my arm stops me. I glance over to see Emerson watching the woman with an amused glint in his eyes.

"My dear woman," he purrs, accent curling around the words. "Trust me that if I wanted your innocent little small town angel she'd already be in the alley with her legs around my waist." He flashes her a razor-sharp smile. "Perhaps it's jealousy that you feel."

The woman's face turns an alarming shade of puce, mouth gaping like a fish out of water. "You—you—you sick man. You're twisted. Depraved."

Wolfgang barks out a reluctant laugh. "Is she trying to insult you?"

Emerson shrugs, tilting his head. "They're compliments, really."

"We don't have time for this," I growl.

Bart emerges from the kitchen, wiping his hands on a dish towel. He frowns at the woman still gaping by the door. "Everything alright out here, Edna?"

Edna's head whips around, eyes narrowing into slits as she takes in Bart. "You! You're on their side, aren't you? Letting these carnie freaks into your establishment!"

Bart looks at us, his expression wary. "You're from the circus."

"Logan Whitmere. I own the circus that came through here a few weeks ago."

A nervous nod. "Good business, good business."

It's good that we have a lead on Sienna, but I won't pass up the opportunity to get more information. That's what we came here for. We don't have any proof that she's at the hunting cabin, but Emerson is right about one thing. Liam already checked Kyle's home. And the room his two friends rent above the hardware store. "I understand Sienna Cole used to work here."

He scratches his head. "She was one of my best workers."

My voice comes out soft. Threatening. "Then I suppose you were unhappy to find out she left. Maybe you decided to get her back."

He begins to swear. "No. I wouldn't." A clatter as he fumbles with a stack of mugs that don't look entirely clean. "Look, she didn't deserve the hate she got around here. I didn't want her to leave, but it was for the best. She was never going to be safe here."

My hands clench into fists. I want to fight invisible threats. Instead I'm faced with this weakling who paid her pennies for her work. "Then why didn't you defend her?"

"You don't know what it's like. People didn't like her for the way she looked. For who she was. They made up stories about her fucking all the guys." He trails off when he sees my expression. A heavy sigh. "I knew it was bullshit, because I was one of the guys who wanted to fuck her. Would've given her a hell of a lot more than eight dollars an hour if she would've let me. I'm not proud of it, but like I said, it's for the best that she left."

A snarl rumbles in my chest, anger burning hot and bright. To think of Sienna enduring the cruelty of these small-minded bigots, alone and afraid, it's almost too much to bear. She deserved so much better than this. "Have you seen her in the past forty-eight hours?"

"No."

"What about Kyle Moore?"

"No, I swear it. If he did something, I had nothing to do with it."

Emerson's hand finds my shoulder, grip firm and grounding. I draw in a sharp breath, struggling to rein in my tumultuous emotions.

"I know," Emerson says softly. "But we need to stay focused. Sienna needs you."

He's right. I close my eyes briefly, letting the steadiness of Emerson's support soothe my frayed nerves. Which is ironic, of course, because he caused this.

Then again, I can't blame him.

It was me.

I'm the one who caused this.

If I'd never sent her away from the circus, she would still be there, telling fortunes in the tent. When I open them again, the rage has receded to a simmering heat, ready to ignite at the slightest provocation but no longer in danger of consuming me whole.

I nod at Emerson, gratitude in my eyes. "Let's go."

Together, we stride out of the café into the bright sunlight. Today, we make things right. Today, we save Sienna. Kyle doesn't stand a chance. Not against all of us, united with a single purpose: to save Sienna, no matter the cost.

We pile into our rental. I take the front passenger seat while Emerson slides into the back, leaning forward between the two front seats.

"The hunting cabin is our best lead right now," Wolfgang says.

Emerson shows us a document on his phone that has coordinates. "I lied about fucking to get the information. My lead was actually the new clown you picked up from here. His mom works at City Hall. I called back to the switchboard and asked him to hook me up."

At this point, I don't care who fucked who. I study the map. It's a small stamp of land along with vague markings of a building. "Emerson, you circle around to the back of the building. Wolfgang, you take the west side. I'll go through the front entrance."

Wolfgang nods, face set in grim determination.

Emerson flicks a mocking salute, though his usual smirk is absent.

"Be careful," I warn them. "We have no idea what we might encounter in there. Kyle already proved he's violent. And that he has friends. Sienna's safety is our top priority."

"Don't worry, boss man," Emerson drawls. "We'll get the girl out safely. And murder the Assholes. All in a day's work for the daring cast of the Cirque des Miroirs."

Wolfgang snorts. Trust Emerson to lighten the mood. But his reassurance, as flippant as it may seem, settles my nerves. Together, we can overcome any challenge.

We've always been strongest as a team.

As we near the cabin, I breathe deep, summoning my courage. Whatever awaits us, we're ready. We fight for those who can't fight for themselves.

And this time, we fight for Sienna.

This time, we fight for truth.

Except when I burst through the door of the cabin, she's not there.

Instead, we find it empty.

It's clear that people have been here, that

someone was kept in this bed, rope around their wrists. But there's no sign of anyone. They're gone.

CHAPTER ELEVEN

Sienna

'VE LIVED IN Forrester all my life, but there are places I haven't been.

I suppose you could say it's lack of interest, a decided dearth of exploration instincts inside me. The truth is, I've always known I'm not welcome here, that the relative safety of town evaporates quickly the further into the forest I get, the deeper into the woods I go.

And that's exactly where I am, as I stumble around, dehydrated, starving, exhausted, battered. I'm worse off now that I've been slapped by about a hundred trees, their stinging branches leaving little red marks across my sunburned skin.

There's something strangely reassuring about the way birds continue trilling and hopping around, searching for worms or mates, doing whatever birds do, entirely unalarmed by the presence of a bedraggled, wandering human.

I'm much more disturbed by my three-second encounter with a doe, its eyes startled and vacant, its tail up with alarm. We stare in each other's general direction, and it's too much like looking in a mirror. We're both prey, after all, both being hunted.

If I were a cartoon princess, I could probably convince the mice and the birds and the deer to lead the way to safety, probably singing cheerfully as they do it. But in the real world, they're all more concerned with their survival than my own.

And so I trudge forward, wincing at the ache in my feet.

At a large clearing, I pause.

I see lush, rolling, manicured hills, only artfully spotted with trees.

It looks like a park, except it's not a park that I recognize, certainly not the center of town, not one of the schools' yards. Where the hell am I? I squint. It is not the small rectangles that clue me in. It's the flowers beside them, bright, garish, plastic flowers in little holders.

I'm at Forrester's Cemetery.

Which means I'm not particularly close to

town.

There's a groundskeeper, I think, but I don't think someone is on site all the time. I wonder if they have an office that I can pilfer. What I wouldn't do for a bottle of water right now, clean water, not the murky stuff I have seen in puddles along the way.

As I go deeper into the cemetery, I come upon a gravel path.

Civilization at last, even if it's only occupied by the deceased.

I've never actually been here in the daytime.

Never attended a funeral here.

When Maisie's grandfather passed away, they had a private, family-only ceremony. I attended the wake at their house after.

By the time Travis's aunt died, we had already lost contact.

My own family has only ever consisted of three people: me, my mother, and my father. My father is dead now, he died the night I left Forrester.

That fact still feels hazy, shrouded in a sense of unreality.

I should be focused on finding the groundskeeper's cottage for food or water.

Or I should keep walking west, because now

at least I know which way Forrester is.

Instead, I become determined.

There's a pull inside me.

Find it, find it, find my father's grave, as if to prove that he's really gone. That the monster of my childhood can't ever come back to haunt me, even if I have plenty of monsters still above ground.

There were a few Halloween nights where we dared each other to go into the cemetery, the moon high above us, giddy with terror. It loomed large in my memory, a dark place, a scary place, a haunted place. But in the sunlight with birds trilling, it feels almost charming, a little sweet, bittersweet.

I search down the paths where the headstones seem smaller, but also newer, and then I find it at the very end of the row, probably the last plot to have gone in. It's still mostly dirt, only a few small sprouts of grass, unlike the others which are covered in thick, lush blades. *Patrick William Cole*, it reads. There is no epitaph, no beloved husband and father, which is fitting for my father. The most notable thing about him is that he was alive, and then one day he was not.

I dropped to my knees beside the grave, shaken by a sense of grief. Not grief for the man who backhanded me from the earliest time I can remember, but grief for a father that I never had. The father who cared about me, the father who protected me, grief that I could never even grieve that man's death because he never existed. He was only ever a dream. I protected myself. I looked down at my arms covered in scratches, I can't say that I've done a wonderful job, only the best that I could.

Tears tickle the skin on my chin as they fall and fall, landing on the broken earth. Some rebellious part of me doesn't want to cry for him, doesn't want him to deserve it, his daughter mourning at his grave. Shouldn't I be happy that he's gone? Shouldn't I be happy that I've had my revenge? Only, I feel empty inside. I'm not glad he's gone, that he's punished, that he suffered, even if I want to be.

Instead, I'm filled with a deep, endless melancholy. Why did it have to be that way? How hard would it have been for him to not hit me, for him to tell me he was proud of me, just once? Such small things, such a low fucking bar. Even with such little expectation he continued to dig his hole deeper, only to end up in an early grave.

I grieve for the father he never was, and for the daughter I had to be.

And then the grief changes. It morphs.

It becomes acceptance.

I am not the daughter he tried to turn me into: fearful, obedient, cowering.

I'm strong, even with bruises on my skin. Even with hunger in my stomach. He couldn't take my humanity. He couldn't take my strength. He couldn't take my dignity.

I escaped again and again.

And fucking again.

More than I should have had to, but that's not a reflection of me.

It's not my job to convince men not to hurt me. It's their job to be human. Not to let themselves turn into monsters, regardless of what society tells them is acceptable.

With that acceptance comes a sense of peace.

The terrible litany of: what did I do to deserve this? What should I have done to avoid it? Nothing, nothing. The world isn't kind to the powerless. I didn't choose it, but I did survive. I made myself stronger. And maybe most importantly, I never became a monster myself.

I feel so peaceful in this moment, so whole, that the sound of an engine almost doesn't register, until it does, and shock rams through my system. A truck, someone's coming, whether it's the groundskeeper coming to mow the lawn or someone coming to visit, they can help me.

They will help me, right?

I have enough fear built up in this town not to be sure. There are people who would spit on me before they let me in their car.

I have to pray that this isn't one of them.

I stand, wondering which direction the sound is coming from. It seems to echo off the trees all around me. And then I don't need to wonder anymore, because a dark SUV tears over the peaceful terrain. Its tires squeal to a stop, my heart thuds. What if it's Kyle? What if it's the Assholes? What if it's Kyle and the Assholes? Even though this car is way too fancy for them to have, anything is possible. I take a step back, prepared to run back into the forest if I need to. Maybe I'll manage the woodland creature army after all. They'll stand and fight for me.

The driver's side door opens, and Logan steps out. Logan Whitmere, owner of Cirque des Miroirs. He should be thousands of miles away right now with the circus, driving to the next town, managing hundreds of people, bringing in thousands every night. What the hell is he doing here, in Forrester, in a freaking cemetery? His expression is unlike any I've ever seen before, darker even than when he kicked me out of the circus, more severe than lightning in the night sky. He looks like the leader of some sort of conquering army, but the only thing he's conquering is a wilted, tired woman. A woman tired of running, tired of surviving, tired of having to be strong.

When he reaches me, I let myself go. This isn't the time to wonder how he found me or what this means for the future. This is an oasis, a dream, a moment where I have everything I need, even if none of it's real. He holds me carefully. His muscles restrained against the hard grasp I can tell he wants to use. His hands roam over me, checking for injuries, pausing at each bruise and each cut.

"You are hurt," he says, his voice like rocks rubbing together.

I force a lopsided smile, "I've been worse." That's not the right answer. His eyes look bloodshot. He looks like he wants to tear the world apart. He forces a hard swallow, and then he lifts me up as easily as if I weigh nothing. Somehow in his arms, I feel like I weigh nothing, like I'm made of air, like he's the earth itself, cradling the atmosphere in his firm grasp.

"Hospital," he says, and out of the corner of

my eye, I see Wolfgang.

"No," I say, my voice hoarse. I know the nurse who works there and how she likes to pinch the children when the grown-ups aren't looking. And worse, I know the doctor. He's so ancient, he probably thinks bloodletting is an appropriate treatment.

Logan hesitates, "You need to be seen."

"I just need…" It's impossible to name everything that I need, especially when my throat is so dry. I need food and water and bandages. "I need to sleep," I say. "You would think 16 hours in a trunk would give a girl time to nap, but surprisingly, no. What can I say? I'm like the princess and the pea, the slightest bump in the road, and I kept waking up."

He drops his head, his forehead touching mine. "You're making jokes."

"Not funny ones. You weren't laughing."

"Sienna," he says, "What am I going to do with you?"

"Not take me to the hospital, hopefully."

He sighs. Then he tells Wolfgang, "North Security." Then the vehicle is moving.

A water bottle appears in his hand, and there can't be anything better, nothing sweeter, not even honey. As the cool liquid pours down my throat, my stomach rebels, and I cough. Logan pulls the bottle away, regretful. "Take it slow, Sunset." I flinch at the nickname, the old nickname, Sunset. Why did I find it romantic? Why did I find it sweet? It just means the end of something, doesn't it? That's all I ever am: an ending, a goodbye.

He sees my reaction, of course. Logan has always seen everything. "Not everything," a voice whispers. He didn't see the truth.

His breath catches, "Sienna, I know what happened."

"Don't," I say.

His eyes burn. "Later then."

There will be no later. Nothing comes after the sunset. Only a long, dark night. That's my last thought before sleep claims me. Because even though my brain tells me that I can't trust this man, that he betrayed me just like everyone else, my body feels differently, it feels safe. And finally, sleep takes me. It drags me under, hands like underwater weeds holding me down, making everything murky.

In that liminal space I hear his voice, though I'm never sure whether he's actually speaking or if it's just part of the dream.

"I'll take care of you," he says, "I'll protect

you, that's a promise. I'm never letting you go."

Those words fill a hole inside me, against my will, against my wishes. I don't want to trust him. I can't trust him. But somewhere deep inside, I already believe.

CHAPTER TWELVE

Logan

I MET LIAM North through our resident knife thrower, Wolfgang. They were both in the military, though neither likes to talk about it. I get the impression they both did black ops. Things that the government ordered them to do but would not like to claim in public. Things that make their records blacked out and confidential.

Wolfgang left the military and decided to join the circus rather than continue in some sort of violent capacity. He prefers to play with a knife's edge. To make audiences gasp with fear and with delight when he manages to avoid someone's head and hit an apple sitting on top of it.

In contrast, Liam North lives a different life. He started the top security firm in the country.

North Security provides bodyguard services to celebrities and politicians alike. I get the impression they're also tapped by the military to do some of those black ops when they want even more plausible deniability about their involvement.

Regardless, the firm is hugely successful and their operations base is only an hour south of Forrester. The way that I use the firm is really too small potatoes for them, but they do it as a favor to me. It mostly has involved helping to track down my half siblings, left from my father, half siblings like Travis, who I approach and offer them a place in the circus if they want it.

They also help me keep tabs on Alessandra whenever she goes off the grid. Usually we're able to track her down, this time has taken longer.

Over the years, Liam has become something of a friend. There are barracks in the compound that he could put us in. Instead, he greets us at the front door of his mansion. I carry a sleeping Sienna in my arms as he leads the way to a suite of rooms.

"We have a medic on site," he says. His green eyes hard as he studies the young woman in my arms. "I can send him up." I spy a first aid kit on a marble table.

"Let me take a look at her first. I'll call down if we need help." He takes in the scratches across her arms and legs. Those emerald eyes meet mine and he nods once. I read in it the same promise that I have felt since the moment I saw her gone. Retribution. There would be punishment for what was done to her as soon as I find out the full extent of it.

I reached down and place a kiss on her forehead as Liam gently shuts the door behind him. "Wake up, Sunset."

Drowsy, brown eyes open. Exhaustion weighs down her lids. I wish I could let her sleep, but I need to understand the full extent here.

"Logan?" she says, her voice drowsy.

"I'm here, Sunset, and I'm going to help you get better. I just need you to be awake for a little while longer and then you can rest."

I carry her into a bathroom that's bigger than most bedrooms. There is a large claw-foot tub, easily fitting two people. There's a standing shower with a bench inside, mirrors everywhere, and plush heated mat beneath our feet. The heat is definitely an extravagance here in Texas, but welcome right now as I have to set her down. There's a velvet bench that she can sit on and I lay her there waiting to see if she's steady before I step back and retrieve the first aid kit.

She holds up her arms, palms down, studying the bruises and the scratches on them. Those look painful enough, but I am afraid to find out what's beneath the clothing. If I had taken her to a hospital, they would've done a rape kit. There would've been DNA. I don't need DNA samples in order to exact justice. I'm going to do it the circus way, the black ops way. Not through the broken legal system that allowed this to happen to her in the first place. That allowed her to be tormented her entire life.

"Where does it hurt the most?" I ask.

Her eyes are solemn. She takes my hand, large between her smaller ones, and presses it against the middle of her chest. "Here," she says.

My rib cage squeezes tight and I fall to my knees in front of her, still holding my hand against her beating heart. Thump, thump, thump. I could have lost her. The entire world could have lost her. The wonder of her snuffed out because bad men are allowed to do bad things.

It infuriates me. It always has infuriated me, but I couldn't fix the world. I couldn't save the world. I could only save one woman, one circus, one community, and so I made that my life's mission and almost lost her in the process.

"I am sorry." I say. "I'm sorry I didn't believe you. I'm sorry that I let you down. I'm sorry that I became just another man who betrayed you in a long line of them."

The corner of her mouth lifts in a sad smile, "But you came back." I don't deserve her absolution and she isn't offering it.

"I am going to undress you," I say. "I need to find out where you're hurt."

She looks away, clearly reluctant. Anyone would be. She's already so exposed. I don't want to make it harder for her, but I also can't let her be untreated. I force the words out through my clenched throat. "There's a medic here, a professional. I can have them sent up instead of me."

"No," she says. "No strangers."

"I won't touch you anywhere, except to help, do you believe me?" Trust. It's not that I deserve trust, it's just that I need to have it if I'm going to help her. After a pause, she nods.

I reached for her shirt and lift it up. Already, she looks thinner. It's only been forty-eight hours since I saw her last but dehydration, lack of nourishment have already changed the shape of her body, even a little bit.

I grit my teeth and force myself to continue,

helping her tug down her jeans until she's naked on the bench. Her limp body, so beautiful and strong, now marred with bruises and cuts. Her limbs curled in on themselves as if she's shielding herself from me, from the world. Her skin has always been a beautiful tan color. Even the parts where the sun can't reach, but there's a darker spot on the inside of her left breast. A mark where *he* must have squeezed.

I can't help the rage that comes over me, even though I warned myself, I told myself to be calm. That I needed to be professional. That I needed to stay collected if I'm going to help her. The sight still fills me with a fury that makes my fists shake at my sides.

"Who?" I say. I already know the answer. It's Kyle and the Assholes, but I want to know which ones of them were involved specifically, and if anyone else was involved because they're all going to die.

She swallows hard. "Don't, please. I can't."

I want to force her to talk to me. I want answers, damn it. But I need to help her more.

"All right." I say, my voice calmer. Forcing the red back from my vision. "You don't have to talk about it now, not who did it, but I need to know if they hurt you inside anywhere. If they…"

"No," she says, her voice a little stronger, her eyes meeting mine. "They didn't fuck me, if that's what you're asking."

She says it that way to be strong, to show me that she's strong, but her voice wavers on the word fuck. Of course, she's still strong regardless, but it shows how afraid she's been, the fear that she's lived under, and the bruise proves that they've at least assaulted her. Even if they didn't go all the way. That can have just as much impact, just as much trauma.

"So goddamn sorry," I whisper.

"Hey," she says, "You didn't do it."

"Didn't I?"

She lifts up her feet showing the mud and scratches blurred together. "I'd really love to get in that shower."

I look back at the whole expanse of marble, beautiful and dangerous to someone who isn't steady on their feet. "I'll go in with you."

Her dark eyes are a mystery, an expanse.

"In your clothes?" She asks, curiously.

"If you'll feel more comfortable that way." I don't even laugh. Ruining a good pair of jeans won't make me feel better.

I strip off my T-shirt, my boots, my socks, my jeans, I leave on my boxer briefs. Her eyebrows lift at the semi that I'm sporting.

"Kinky," she says.

I growl low in my throat. "It doesn't mean anything. It's just looking at your body would do this to me anytime. Nothing is going to happen in that shower."

"Are you sure?" she asks.

"Absolutely sure."

"Then that's a disappointment," she states. "I wanted to be clean in every way possible. Body, soul. I think you can help me do that."

Naturally, my erection goes to full mast, excited by the possibility of helping her in whatever way possible, and of course getting off in the process. What a helpful, unselfish bastard I am.

"Sunset, you aren't…"

"I'm not what? Pure enough? Clean enough? Unblemished enough?"

"You've been through something terrible," I say. "You've been hurt. You've been held captive. What you need is rest, food, water, medicine. What you need is peace. And then if you still want me, I'm yours."

She swallows hard. "So you would take away my consent? My ability to consent?"

I curse long and low under my breath. It's a hell of a conundrum. If she wants me, I'm not sure I have the power to say no.

Emotion chooses that moment to overwhelm her.

Grief. Regret. Rage.

All of it comes pouring over her, hotter and harder than the shower.

She sobs, and I hold her.

I hold her because that's the only thing I can do.

She's damn near catatonic by the time the last sob seeps from her. I move her limbs as if she's a doll, cleaning her free of dirt and blood. Then I tend her wounds with ointment. By the time I tuck her into the plush bed, she's already asleep.

Part of me longs to climb in beside her, to watch her dream.

The other part of me knows I have to go.

There's work to be done.

I step outside and close the door.

Footsteps come up behind me. I whirl, muscles tensed, only to find Liam leaning against the balcony. My friend's gaze holds a mixture of emotions: concern, protectiveness, and no small amount of warning.

"Are you sure you don't want help?"

I shake my head. "You don't need to be caught up in this."

"You need to be careful," he says quietly. "If the authorities find out—"

"They won't." My voice comes out harsh, grating. I take a breath and try again. He's offering to help me take revenge on Kyle, but I can't accept. I can't risk his company's reputation or his contacts with law enforcement. "I'll be careful. I'm in control."

"Are you?" Liam's stare bores into me, seeing too much. "Sienna isn't the only one with wounds that need healing. You can't just pretend the past isn't part of you."

"Watch me." I turn away, dismissing him.

Right now my focus must remain on Sienna. On keeping her safe. On proving I'm worthy of the gift I want more than my next breath: her trust.

Liam hesitates a moment longer before retreating down the hall, his footsteps echoing into silence. Alone at last, I settle into the chair beside Sienna's bed, keeping vigil through the remaining hours of night.

Come dawn, our future will begin anew.

Between now and then I have a task to complete.

CHAPTER THIRTEEN

Logan

M Y PLANS FOR a quiet escape are dashed by the sight of men lounging against the SUV.

Emerson raises an eyebrow as if challenging me.

I glance at Wolfgang, who shrugs.

"We'll make him go first," he says. "In case they're armed."

"Come, mon ami." Emerson strolls over. "After all we've been through? We do this together."

"You can watch." It's the only concession I'm going to make.

"Gladly," Wolfgang says. "I have a feeling you'll need witnesses."

A short nod before I climb into the driver's

seat.

My fingers tighten around the steering wheel as I speed down the winding country roads. Anger simmers in my gut, fueled by the memory of Sienna's bruised and battered face.

How could I let this happen? I should have protected her.

The bonfire is visible a mile away, sparks flying high into the sky before going out. Next comes the bass of music being played from someone's truck. Only when I pull up on a rise do I see the crowd of people lounging on a pebbled beach and dark lake. *Found you.*

I pull up beside the cars and step out.

It doesn't take long to find him, surrounded by friends.

I don't nod toward Maisie even though she's the one who sent me the text alerting me to Kyle's location. No reason these assholes need to know that.

His eyes widen in surprise before he schools his expression, pretending indifference, pretending he's not afraid. "What the hell do you want?"

"To have a conversation," I say, as if a conversation means death, "about Sienna."

Kyle hesitates, then puts down his beer. "What about her?"

"About where she got those bruises."

His eyes darken in the firelight. "That's none of your concern."

I keep my voice low, even though we're surrounded by people. They're watching. Witnesses. That's important. "Because she's yours. That's what you think, right?"

His jaw clenches. He definitely still wants her. "You think you know her? She's been mine since we were in fucking kindergarten. Back the hell off."

"I don't think so," I say, my voice still low. "Not with the number of ways I've had her. I know how she tastes when she comes. Do you know how sweet she tastes, Kyle?"

Fury makes him turn red. "Shut up, motherfucker. Right now."

"And the way she sucks cock." I force myself to remember the feel of her mouth, the impossible warmth, the magic of her even in the presence of this scum. To make it realistic. "She's the best I ever had. But not the best you've ever had, is it? Because you've never had her. She never let you have her. You had to kick her, someone half your weight, punch her in the face, just to hold her."

His friends have come to back him up. Good. "You don't know the danger you're in," he spits.

"This isn't your little fucking carnival. This is Forrester, and we protect our own."

"The way you protected Sienna?"

There it is, that flicker of guilt. The sliver of humanity. The memory of the little boy who was once friends with her. It's quickly subsumed by the monster he's become. "If she had only listened to me, this never would have happened."

I smile. It's a cruel smile. I imagine it's the one my birth father saw before he held my mother down. Pure cruelty. Only the animal side of me is left. "I'm going to enjoy this."

"Get him," he says, huffing a harsh breath.

That sends one of the Assholes toward me. I vaguely remember from the file that this one is Randall Todd, the one who owns the hunting cabin that was empty. Doesn't matter. The way Sienna names them makes more sense. Asshole #1 and Asshole #2.

The first one comes at me, a glint in his dark eyes. He enjoys the fight.

I slam a fist into his face. It hurts me more than it does him. Great.

My body has been through a thousand fights. And more than that, it's carried the equipment for a circus from city to city for countless shows. I'm tall and strong and experienced, but these guys still have about one hundred pounds on me of pure mass.

Better rely on experience, then.

Which means I need to use his own weight against him. Asshole #2 doesn't wait for his turn. He comes at me with a kind of plodding charge, his expression more determined than gleeful. I whip around, sweeping low, so that he trips directly into the fist Asshole #1 aimed at me.

They both go down in a painful-sounding thud of heavy bodies.

The crowd laughs. A good thing because I need people on my side.

They're witnesses for what comes next.

Important witnesses.

This is what Wolfgang meant on the way here. See, killing people is legal. There's a loophole, though. A technicality. Self-defense.

Which means they see Kyle throw the sucker punch.

They see him come toward me when he thinks I'm not looking.

Except I was waiting for this. I *wanted* this, because then whatever I do next will be self-defense. When I kill him, it will be legal.

I have experience with murder, after all.

He lands the punch, and my brain rattles. I

stumble back, letting my body absorb the impact fully. It hurts, but not as badly as what I'm about to do to him. Besides, I deserve it. This punch was for not believing Sienna. At least that's what it means to me.

I stagger back to standing, not bothering to hide the wince. Better that they see it. Another punch will cement this as self-defense. Three men against one. And this one, Kyle, punching me for no apparent reason, while I stand still, my hands at my side.

This one blasts my jaw. Hurts like a motherfucker.

Deserve it. I deserve it.

Not for what Kyle thinks, of course. Not for taking away Sienna. I'd do that a thousand times over again, even if it earned me a place in eternal damnation.

And, well, it probably will.

I deserve it for losing her, for letting her be taken.

For the bruise on her breast.

The memory crystallizes my purpose here.

My eyes narrow. Two punches is enough, right?

"One more, mon ami," comes the low murmur from Emerson.

A cautious man, perhaps.

But correct.

The third punch knocks me on my ass. The entire crowd watches with held breath as their town golden boy, the town bully beats up a stranger. Some people have even taken their phones out. Good. Video evidence will go further than eyewitnesses, anyway.

When I stand, there's a sense of peace.

I've grappled with violence my whole life, but here, tonight, it doesn't feel like a conflict. It feels like purpose. I throw a punch at Kyle, who immediately crumples. He didn't expect me to hit back. And with his two Assholes he probably doesn't get hit very often.

I wait for him to stand up before hitting him again, but this time when he falls, I go down with him. A natural-looking tumble, one that allows me to straddle him, to slam my fist into his face. Again. And again. That handsome all-American face, the one that could have pulled any girl except for the one he wanted to possess.

No one will call him handsome after this.

I feel his jaw break under my fist.

A tooth comes loose.

He moans and moves his hands loosely.

Mostly I have tunnel vision but some small

part of me is aware of the crowd watching, of their silence, of their shock as they watch the town bully get systematically destroyed.

Even the Assholes have stood up now, and they watch in shock.

Maybe they saw Kyle as some kind of god. Untouchable.

No, he's just human. He's just another asshole.

One who's going to die tonight.

I hit him again and again and again, until he's slumped against the ground, battered and bloody. Even now I will not stop. I hear Sienna's voice in my head, calling for mercy, but it must be a mirage. This man didn't give her mercy, so why would he deserve it?

No, I need to kill him. Kill. Kill. Kill.

Blinding lights pull me up short. I stand up off Kyle's limp, still-breathing body with reluctance just in time to greet the state trooper who once inquired about Alessandra's whereabouts. He raises an eyebrow. "Mr. Whitmere. It seems like whenever there's trouble, you're there."

CHAPTER FOURTEEN

Sienna

I N MY DREAMS, I envision a grand circus tent filled with life-sized dolls, their movements controlled by invisible strings, creating a surreal and magical atmosphere.

I'm standing in the center of an enormous circus tent, dazzled by the spectacle surrounding me. Graceful dolls spin and twirl through the air, dancing as if on invisible strings. Their movements are fluid and precise, creating a surreal, dreamlike atmosphere.

As I watch, mesmerized, one doll breaks free of the intricate ballet. She floats down until we're face-to-face, her porcelain features exquisite. But where her eyes should be are empty sockets, dark and fathomless.

A shiver runs down my spine at the sightless gaze. The doll's lips curve into a knowing smile and she whispers in a voice like rustling silk, "He's not who you think he is."

I jerk awake with a gasp, blinking against the darkness. Just a dream, I tell myself. But the doll's warning lingers, sowing seeds of doubt in my mind.

I blink, disoriented. For a moment I expect to see the modern interior of Logan's RV. Then it comes rushing back—the compound, Kyle, Logan. I glance at the clock on the nightstand. I've been asleep for over twelve hours.

My gaze falls to a tray on a wooden table, laden with food and a vase of fresh flowers. There are bright red poppies and yellow mums and thick sprigs of lavender. A note propped against the vase catches my eye.

Eat. Don't get up without help.

– Logan

My stomach rumbles at the scent of spice, but hesitance weighs heavy in my gut.

Logan's kindness leaves me wary, his motives unclear.

He vowed to protect me. But can I truly trust him?

Have I traded one cage for another?

The questions swirl through my thoughts as I stare at the shadows, finding no answers in the night. The memory of his hands massaging shampoo into my hair surfaces unbidden. I shake my head, dislodging the image. I can't trust him, no matter how comforting his presence feels.

Still, I have nowhere else to go, and I'm tired of running.

For now, I'll play along.

I rise and pad over to the tray, intending to sample a few bites only. I'm shocked to discover a plate of chicken satay on wooden sticks, nicely browned over a fire, still juicy and vibrant. They rest on a bed of jasmine rice sprinkled with saffron.

It's an Indonesian dish.

I don't know the name of it, but my mother has made ones like it a thousand times. There is even a small bowl filled with peanut sauce for dipping.

My curiosity turns into rampant hunger.

Suddenly, I'm starving. Not only for protein and sustenance. I'm starving for the reminder of home. Even so close to Forrester I don't feel like I belong. Even with my mother nearby this is not my land. It's in the food, the flavors, the spices.

It's in the care that went into preparing this dish especially for me.

A soft knock sounds at the door.

"Sienna? Are you awake?" A feminine voice is muffled but laced with concern.

"Yes, come in." I school my features into indifference, bracing myself as the door opens.

"Feeling better?" It's a young woman who looks startlingly similar to myself. A round face. Dark hair and eyes. Full lips. Tan skin. Her sympathetic gaze travels over me, assessing, as she steps closer to the bed. "I'm Samantha. There are fresh clothes in the wardrobe and toiletries in the bathroom."

I nod, swallowing back my request for Logan. "Thank you."

"I thought you might want a visitor."

Alarm runs through me because I'm in no shape to meet anyone new right now. Samantha seems nice enough, calm enough, but I'm not really up for meeting new people. But it's not a person who runs through the door. It's the dog.

"Oh, God," I say, dropping to my knees.

He runs into my arms, and I hold his quivering body close to my heart.

"You're okay. You're okay," I murmur against his face as he licks my lips, my nose, my eyelids. "I was so afraid for you." He licks me back, frantic as if to tell me, *I was afraid for you too.*

Samantha's eyes are warm as she watches us. "He's been such a well-behaved little boy. Comes when he's called. Sits. Lies down. He can even roll over."

"What?" I say, pulling back with surprise. An unexpected smile on my face. "Is that true? Can you roll over? Let me see."

To prove the point. He rolls onto his back and then stands back up with a spring in his step. His tan fur looks none the worse for the wear after our adventure, after the long drive that he must have done to get here.

His one ear flaps down while the other one points up, making him look perpetually jaunty. He pants at me, looking cheerful.

"Good boy," I murmur, scratching him behind those ears. "What a good boy."

"Your friends brought him," Samantha says, "I wasn't sure if I should wake you up."

"My friends?"

"Travis and Maisie."

"Oh," I hold the dog close to me, while my chest clenches. Maisie has been a good friend to me, loyal, trustworthy. I love her dearly, but I also can't imagine coming back to live in Forrester after I left, after being dragged back against my will. I can't go back to working at the coffee shop like nothing happened. But I also have nowhere else to go. I don't belong here, but I also don't belong in the circus anymore, which is where Travis is.

"They were worried about you," Samantha says, softly.

I look down and breathe in deep, taking in that puppy musk along with dirt that he's accumulated across thousands of miles. It feels as refreshing as a summer breeze, as sweet as a rose, because it's him, because he's safe and because now that I can take a break, take a breath, I know that I'm safe too.

"I appreciate you letting me sleep," I say, "and for bringing me this little guy. Do you live here?"

She gives me a soft smile. "I do. Along with Liam, my husband."

"Oh," I say, not able to hide the surprise in my voice. "It's just that you look like me."

A soft laugh. "I noticed that, and I hope you don't mind that I probed a little and asked Logan about your heritage. I'm from Indonesia too. Though, according to that DNA test I took, there's a decent amount of origin in China, too."

Strange that I've never actually met someone

Indonesian, besides my mother. It feels like a sense of coming home even though she's a stranger. "You took a DNA test?"

"Yeah. I don't know how accurate they are, but I didn't exactly have a good relationship with my mother, so that was the only way I could find out more about where I came from."

I looked down. My mother... I'm not sure you could say we had a good relationship, but it wasn't a bad one either. She was willing to tell me about her childhood, as long as my father wasn't around. As long as she wasn't hiding in her bedroom from the bruises, it was always a painful relationship, a painful life, really. And the worst part is I'm not sure that my father's death actually freed her.

"If you want, I can introduce you to my mom. She usually likes talking about where she came from." Samantha's eyes light up.

"That would be so great." She gestures toward the plate of food. "I look up recipes and read books, but I always feel like an outsider looking in, you know? Which is funny, considering it's me. It's in my genes. It's how I look, it's what I'm made of."

My stomach growls, and I take a bite of the satay. My eyes close against the sheer pleasure.

"Oh my God, that's so good."

She laughs. "I'm going to pretend like that's a real compliment and not just the fact that you've basically been starved."

The dog whines and I give him a little piece. "He likes it too," I say. Samantha laughs.

Then she sobers. "Do you want to rest? Or maybe privacy?"

I feel suddenly shy. I don't have much experience with making friends. "If you have to go, that's fine," I say. "But if you want to hang out, I would enjoy the company."

"Oh, in that case," she says, getting down on the floor with me crossing her legs, and I laugh at her eagerness.

"I'm desperate for another girl," she says. "This place is teeming with men."

I glance around at the elegant surroundings. "Meaning what?"

She laughs. "We can show you later. There's a whole training camp for the security firm my husband runs. All the recruits come through here, and it's like home base and most of the agents are men. I'm the only female, which means a lot of testosterone. I am happy to have a girl around."

"People aren't usually happy to have me around." My cheeks heat. I guess I shouldn't have said that out loud. Her eyes soften.

"I know what it's like not to fit in. I never lived in Forrester, or really even struggled because of my heritage, or the way I look, but the way I played violin from an early age, it marked me. It set me apart from the other kids, and I really struggled to make relationships." She glances down at the dog. "I probably should have gotten one of those."

"I've always wanted one." I say, scruffing up his fur, so he shivers into delight. "But my father…" My voice trails off.

She clearly catches on that it's a bad subject, so she says, "What are you going to name him?"

"Good question. Something circus-y."

"Circus-y, like Barnum & Bailey?"

"That's two names," I say, and we laugh.

She studies him as he runs around, hopping on his hind legs, begging for another piece of the chicken satay.

"I would love to share, but I'm also starving," I say, laughing. "Maybe if you do another trick."

This inspires the dog to sit back on his haunches and wave his paws in the air as if he's begging. Both Samantha and I laugh.

"He really likes doing tricks," she says.

"All right," I say, "I have to give him a reward

for that."

I give him a piece of chicken, which he laps up eagerly. "Maybe that's what I should call him. Tricks."

"That's a cute name," she says, "and he's certainly living up to it. I wonder what else we can teach him?" And her expression falls. "I'm not sure how long you'll stick around, of course, but you're welcome to stay here as long as you need."

"Thank you," I say looking down. "I am not sure that I'll be able to repay you."

"Hey," she says gently, "you don't need to repay us anything. We just want you to be safe."

"Why?" I ask. "I'm a stranger to you."

"Not quite a stranger," she says. "For one thing, you are with Logan. And we like Logan, most of the time, but more than that, I feel like we're kin, you know? Outcasts got to stick together."

The corner of my lips turns up. "That's the motto of the circus, isn't it?"

"Yeah," she says, "that's why we fit in there."

CHAPTER FIFTEEN

Logan

B Y THE TIME I make it back to North Security headquarters, the sun hangs high overhead.

It's almost noon.

I'm alone, Emerson and Wolfgang having departed Forrester's Police Station hours earlier. I walk through the front door and am greeted by the sound of laughter.

Everything that I've experienced over the past twenty-four hours has drained me.

It's drained me of life force, of hope.

And God, this laughter, it fills me back up.

I follow the sound as if in a trance and stand at the door of a large sitting room.

Sienna is on the floor, her long legs crossed, wearing a dress that I assume she borrowed, something light and flowery, the sea foam green highlighting the beautiful tan of her skin.

There's an expression of pure joy on her face.

It's enough to stop my heart.

What I wouldn't give to see that expression every day of my life.

What I wouldn't give to see that expression directed at me. I'm a selfish bastard at heart. It's not enough that I want her to be happy, I want her to be happy with me, for me, near me.

Her hands are animated as she shows the dog something she wants him to do.

There's a stack of books, thick tomes with cloth bindings on the floor. It looks like she's trying to get him to stand on it.

He puts his front paws on the books and then looks at her expectantly, wagging his little tail, panting, hoping to get some of what looks to be cheese cubes that she's holding in her hand.

"All the way," she says, coaxing. "Come all the way up with your back feet too."

She taps the books to show him what to do.

The little dog hops off and then hops back on, front paws only from a different angle, as if to say, *Is this right?*

"So close," she says, her voice encouraging. And patient. "Come all the way up."

I'm aware of Samantha, Liam's wife, watching and cheering them on, but I can't take my eyes off of Sienna. I suppose to some people, the women might look similar.

They both have black hair and black eyes, beautiful olive tone skin, and slender bodies.

But to me, they couldn't look more different.

Liam's wife is a striking woman, but Sienna is as breathtaking and changeable as the sunset. No one else has those jaded eyes that hide a heart full of hope. No one else has that beautiful mouth that I want to kiss, want to taste, want to breathe through.

No one else has a body that makes me hard just thinking about it.

The visible cuts and bruises I can see from here don't stop my cock from wanting her. Even knowing she's injured, she's tired, she's traumatized, I want to fuck her into the ground.

She nudges the little dog's back feet, tapping them until he pulls them up on top of the pile of books, standing proud on the improvised pedestal.

Sienna whoops and praises him. "What a good boy, such a good boy."

He chomps down happily on his cheese reward.

Samantha also claps, an enthusiastic audience. It's when she's mid-laughter that she notices me. Some of her amusement fades. She stands and says, "I'll give you two a moment."

And then we're alone, Sienna and I.

Sienna's expression turns grave, but there's still a twinkle of amusement at the dog's antics.

She stands and confronts me. "You look a little worse for wear."

I touch a hand to my swollen brow and wince. "Took a few hits."

"Do I want to ask who you've been fighting?"

"Sunset," I say, "I will slay every one of your dragons for you."

"Then it's unfortunate I have so many." Her tone is deadpan.

My eyes close, only this woman could find humor in this situation. I lead her to the couch and sit down. The dog jumps up and sits between us, looking expectant.

She grins. "He wants the cheese in my pocket. I named him, did I tell you that? He's Tricks."

I gently shove Tricks down to the ground. "I need a few moments with her," I tell him.

He looks like he's thinking about arguing, but ultimately goes and sits down, curled up on the pile of books, now that he knows it's a place that brings him treats.

"I'd rather not tell you the details. But you'll find out eventually. I fought with Kyle and the two Assholes."

Her eyes grow dark with emotion. "Where are they now?"

"Not where I want them to be. I was hoping they'd be underground. That was the plan anyway."

"Logan. You can't endanger yourself like that."

A reluctant smile curves my lips. "As I was beating him, I thought I could hear you telling me to stop, though I didn't know why you would grant him mercy."

And this woman, this beautiful, gorgeous, strong, unbreakable woman, laughs. "Mercy? For him? No. But you would get in trouble."

"I had it worked out. He'd hit me three times, it would've been self-defense."

She frowns. "That's still a risk."

I shrug because the risk was meaningless to me. My freedom means nothing, her safety is everything. "If they threw me in jail, I'd probably lead a revolt within six months."

She shakes her head trying to look disapproving but failing. "That much I believe."

"Well, I was stopped before I could finish the job. State Trooper Brian Jones showed up. Apparently you'd called him."

Her eyes widened. "Wow, I wasn't sure that actually happened or that he would even care if he found out."

"Apparently he's been looking for you. He figured out it was Kyle and went to the bonfire to find him, only to find me on top of him, pummeling him."

"Oh, no," she whispers.

"Yeah, I got arrested. Don't worry. Emerson and Wolfgang were with me. They called Cirque des Miroirs' lawyer, who got me out. There was video evidence that proved that Kyle had started it, so he's the one in lockup tonight. I'm free."

"*Logan*," she says, her voice emphasizing her concern. It warms me that concern, even though I don't deserve it. "Promise me you won't go after him."

I shake my head. "I would go after him right now, except that he's in county lockup and it doesn't look like he'll be free anytime soon. Not for what he did to me and not for what he did to you. Jones is coming by later to take your statement."

Tears reflect in her dark eyes. "Okay, I can do

that."

"I'll be right here with you," I tell her. "Jones seems like a standup guy, but if he pushes too hard or asks you anything uncomfortable, I'll protect you."

She sighs. "Maybe I don't want to be someone who needs protection. Maybe I want to defend myself."

I brush the backs of my fingers against her cheek. "We aren't meant to do this alone."

"This?"

"This whole thing, this human experience. We aren't meant to be alone. That's what the circus means. But it's not just true for the circus. It's for towns, it's for cities, it's for companies, it's for families. We're meant to have support and your support should have been protecting you from predators like your father and Kyle all along. You didn't fail by getting hurt. They failed you."

Her eyes close. "Part of me thinks that's true and the other part of me thinks maybe I just should have been stronger."

"Stronger?" I ask. A rough laugh coming out of me. "You're the strongest woman I've ever met, the strongest person I've ever met. If you got any stronger, you would be made of pure liquid gold, burning hot and immutable."

Her eyes are luminous as she looks up at me. "You're the only person who sees me that way."

"Then everyone else is blind," I murmur.

And then she's kissing me.

I don't know whether it's because she pushed up from the sofa or whether it's because I leaned down or both at the same time. We meet in a hard press of need, of heart pounding desire.

This isn't like the shower when she wanted me to erase something that had been done to her. This is something else. It's about seeing to the heart of her. It's about letting her see into the heart of me. About our bodies matching what our minds are already doing, melding, merging, loving, wanting, feeling.

My hands roam beneath the dress and find her wearing no panties. I groan against her lips. "What are you doing to me?"

She shivers in my arms. "I didn't mind borrowing a dress, but it felt a little weird to borrow underwear. I talked to my mom on the phone, she's bringing some of my stuff later."

"I like this better," I say, my voice low and gravelly.

I drop down to my knees in front of her, she's still sitting on the sofa and I spread her legs.

The dress hangs low between them, covering

her up, and so it's like a gift. A gift that I get to unwrap slowly, lifting the fabric until I see her spread like an offering for me.

I look up and see the darkened blush on her cheeks.

"Tell me you want this." Not because I doubt it, her arousal is clear from her body, her expression, from the slickness that glistens against her sex.

But I want her to know that I'm taking this only because she's giving it to me.

I want that to be clear.

"Yes," she murmurs. "Logan, yes."

I swallow hard. Trust. Fucking trust.

My hands are braced on her thighs, pushing her wider, so that I can bend down and give her a kiss. The most intimate kind of kiss, so that I can lick her from the very bottom to the top, lingering at her clit, swooping a circle with my tongue.

I go back down to her entrance, my cock throbs in my pants, wanting inside, but it won't get there. Not now, maybe not ever.

But I can give her this pleasure, for herself alone.

I can lick her folds where she's most sensitive. Make her come on the sofa.

"Someone could…" she says, breathless.

"Someone could come in."

"They won't. Samantha knows better. She's married to Liam North after all."

Sienna shivers in my arms, and I set about making it worse. I want her to shudder, I want her to writhe. I want her to cling to the sofa as if she's dying.

And so I suck her clit and put two fingers inside her. I curl them, finding that secret spot that makes her jerk, that makes her groan.

"Please," she moans. "*Please.*"

And yes, God, yes, anything, everything.

One hand squeezes her ass, holding her close to my face, the other fingers her unrelenting, merciless. And when she comes, it's with the rush of evening rain, a cleansing, a baptizing. Her arousal slick against my lips, delicious to taste. I lap at her through her orgasm, drinking it down, desperate for more, until she's all the way on the other side, too sensitive, slinking away from my caress. She's boneless in my hold as I return to sit on the couch and hold her on my lap. My cock throbs, it wants her and it would be so easy to have her, she wouldn't resist. But the truth is, I don't deserve that, in a way—in a strange, perverse, self-flagellation way—I don't even want it.

I can make her come a thousand more times without ever having satisfaction, the blue balls my personal penance. She wriggles on my lap, feeling the erection.

"What about you?" she asks.

What about me? That's the question. Where do we go from here? This woman who's been imprisoned in a thousand different ways, she deserves to be free. She deserves to make her own choices. Where do I fit into that? Maybe nowhere. Maybe everywhere, and I'm not going to fuck her again until she's mine.

I press a kiss to her temple. "Don't worry about me."

She laughs, the sound a little watery, a little desperate. "I wish I could stop, but you seem to keep getting into trouble."

My lips curve. "It's nothing I can't handle. I'm focused on you, what you need, what you want. That's it."

She pulls back and looks me in the eye. "Then take me to bed."

I have her halfway up the stairs when the doorbell rings.

CHAPTER SIXTEEN

Sienna

KYLE AND THE Assholes are in jail.

They can't come after me again.

They can't hurt me—or anyone else for that matter.

It's hard for me to process, but what's even stranger is that I don't process it alone.

State Trooper Brian Jones shows up, all professionalism at least until I throw my arms around him and burst into tears. It's hard to explain how much it meant that someone was looking for me. Yes, it's because I had someone reach out, but the fact is a lot of people in law enforcement, a lot of people in general could have ignored that call. They could have assumed it was a prank or that it was too hard to figure out where I was since the call was made from a gas station somewhere between here and Arizona. Or they could have assumed the girl was lying to get attention.

"Thank you," I say, my voice raw with emotion.

He blushes, reminding me of the time I first met him, which is when he was in my fortune-teller's tent on a first date, shy and infatuated.

I kind of want to ask him about it, but I don't want to make him feel bad in case it didn't work out because the truth is I can't actually tell the future.

Even though they made an adorable couple.

"We're still together," he says, in answer to my unasked question, he looks pleased as punch with himself, and I can't help but laugh, the sound echoing off the walls of the foyer.

We go into the sitting area, Logan a stalwart supporter at my side. State Trooper Jones asks me questions step-by-step, documenting it all so that it can be used in a trial, something I'm not particularly looking forward to.

At the end, I look away. "Listen, give it to me straight. If this does go to trial, they're going to tear me apart on the stand, right? That's what they always do to women."

His expression darkens. "I understand your

concern. This won't be like that. I promise you. The man will probably cop a deal unfortunately because the DA would rather keep this quiet than have a media circus."

The words media circus make me nauseous.

"However," he says, "we have physical evidence about what they did, including not only your bruises and testimony, but also security camera footage from the gas station."

My eyes widen. "There was a security camera?"

That place did not look like it could afford one. The trooper looks grim. "Unfortunately, human trafficking is not nearly as rare as people think. The back roads see a lot of people being taken and transported against their will."

I shiver remembering the darkness of the trunk. A tall, handsome man with broad shoulders walks into the room with us. His green eyes striking. "And if there is media," Liam says, "We'll provide close security. They won't touch you. They won't get to talk to you, at least not directly."

He introduces himself as Liam North to the State Trooper. Brian appears to recognize his name, and his security firm, North Security, by the subtle straightening of his posture.

Samantha follows her husband inside, her expression pained and empathetic.

It's a pain that all women know. The reality of being torn apart for their past, whether it was real or made up or the fear of it. Or knowing it could happen based on what's happening between their legs, based on their gender, knowing that violence will be excused against their body by so many people who hear about it, and with that I know I'm not alone in this. For some inexplicable reason, I have allies. No, there is an explanation. It's Logan. Logan may have betrayed me that one night, but he has also supported me, helped me, protected me. He's given me these allies. He's given me this hope.

I nod resolutely, "Okay, I can do this."

Samantha sits next to me and squeezes my hand. "Do you need to go lie down or do you want company?"

It's shocking the level of peace that washes over me having someone who cares about my preferences, having someone who's willing to leave me alone or spend time with me based on what I need.

I feel a little shy actually saying it though. "I would love to hang out with you, with all of you."

That's how I end up seated around a large

dinner table, the heady scent of spices—lemongrass, turmeric, and ginger—mingled with the fragrance of coconut milk and freshly ground peanuts.

Liam and Samantha, on either side in this traditional family style, two heads of the table. I'm seated next to Samantha, with Logan on my other side, cocooned in safety.

Maisie showed up in a barrage of hugs and quiet grief for what happened. She's sitting across from me, Wolfgang next to her. There is impressive chemistry going on between them.

Maisie is flirting because she loves to do that.

Wolfgang is acting stoic, but the sparks are hot even across the table.

I whisper to Logan, "What's up with that?"

He leans back. "We met her at the coffee shop. She was helping us find you. She told us about the hunting cabin. They met there though. I don't know what this is about."

"What's the point of making a bed?" Maisie says, "It just becomes unmade that night anyway, it's like a complete waste of time."

Wolfgang's eyes narrow. "It's about discipline. It's about cleaning something up after you've used it."

"How messy does your bed get anyway?"

Maisie challenges, clearly flirting.

Her eyes meet mine across the table and I can't help but smile.

Wolfgang doesn't know what's hit him.

Platters are filled with an array of colorful dishes. A steaming bowl of fragrant beef rendang takes center stage, the tender meat simmered in a rich coconut curry that melts in the mouth. There's a platter of nasi goreng, fried rice, glistening with a medley of shrimp, chicken, and vegetables, topped with a few perfectly fried eggs.

The table also boasts satay skewers, each stick loaded with marinated chicken and grilled to perfection, accompanied by a peanut dipping sauce. The aroma of grilled meats mingles with the sweet and smoky flavors, making the atmosphere lively and inviting. The food provides a pleasant weight in my stomach, a contented lassitude in my limbs.

There are glasses of a sweet iced tea called *es teh*, its caramel hue glistening in the fading sunlight through the tall windows. A sunset glows from beyond the rolling hills.

I feel drunk on good care and laughter.

"When do you go on tour?" Logan asks.

Liam answers. "We had a South American tour, but it's just been canceled."

I glance at Samantha because I know she's a professional violinist, a prodigy actually, and this is a little bit taboo. She was raised by Liam. He was her guardian until he eventually became her friend, her lover, her husband.

"Is everything okay?" I ask her.

She gives me a smile that I can only describe as sly. "It's more than okay. Should we tell them?" she asks her husband. He doesn't answer, just gives her that direct green gaze filled with so much love and so much pride, it almost hurts to watch it. "I'm expecting."

"Oh my God." I can't help myself. I jump up from the table and go hug her.

She squeezes me back whispering to me so that only I hear, "You're going to be her Indonesian auntie." Everyone hugs. The men shake hands before we settle down to start eating dinner.

Samantha talks about her plans for the nursery while Liam gazes at her with admiration. Maisie continues to taunt Wolfgang, getting him worked up. As for me, I'm quiet. Basking in the love and acceptance around the table. I slip tiny pieces toTricks who waits patiently at my feet beneath the table.

"Oh," Maisie says to me, "I have to show you what these new kids graffitied on Forrester High

School. They've been scrubbing for weeks and can't get it off."

I snort because the pranks that people pull on that school are infamous every year like a rite of passage really.

"Maybe we can go to the homecoming game," she says, "Oh, if you'll be here that long."

I look down because I don't even know my plans. I don't know what I'm doing tonight. Much less what I'm doing in a couple weeks from now.

"You can stay as long as you want," Samantha says gently. "I love the company."

"Thank you," I tell her genuinely. "I do appreciate this so much. I want to stand on my own two feet though. I'm just not quite sure how yet."

As if feeling my tension, Tricks licks my ankles from beneath the table. Maisie looks regretful that she brought it up, but I don't want her to feel that way. I appreciate someone treating me like I'm a little bit normal.

"Tell me something else that's going on. Some sort of drama with the Garden Club again."

"Oh you know," she says. "Everyone's freaking out about the circus coming back to town." And then she freezes, realizing what she just said.

"It is not operational right now. I am not

open for business. No shows are happening."
Logan declares.

"We're just camped out. Waiting," Wolfgang adds.

Logan leans back. "It can wait."

Wolfgang and Logan stare at each other and I sense disagreement. I sense tension. Presumably Wolfgang doesn't want to wait. What are they waiting for anyway? Logan can leave whenever he wants."

Liam sets down his fork. "I wasn't sure when to bring this up, but I got a notification right before dinner that Alessandra Gallo has been found."

Anxiety turns my muscles hard as wood. "Where is she? At the fairgrounds?"

Liam nods. "She showed up to her the RV she shared with her daughter. Cat is the one who called us, actually. We still don't know where Alessandra was hiding all this time."

My palms turn sweaty. I clench the arms of the ornate wooden chair. "I may know something about that." Every pair of eyes in the room turns to me. I let myself focus on Logan because I'm overwhelmed. "There's something I have to tell you."

"What is it?"

"It was Alessandra. She's the one who helped Kyle. She's the one who convinced them all to lie"—her eyes close—"and of course she more than anyone knew all about the Ferris wheel and how you would react to it."

His expression turns dark. It turns dangerous.

CHAPTER SEVENTEEN

Logan

MY BLOOD POUNDS, my heart races. It was Alessandra who did this? It hurt enough to know that Emerson, someone I considered my friend, would do this. But in a way it's kind of his modus operandi to cause trouble, and I understand that he was doing what he could to save the circus. I don't forgive it, but I understand it. "She's the one who left."

Sienna straightens her dress, clearly uneasy with my rage. "Apparently she wanted her daughter to be with you. She thought you two could rule the circus together."

"Fuck."

"You're not responsible for her, you know."

"We'll disagree about that. She was part of the

circus. And she hurt you."

I'm making her nervous, her eyes wide. The aroused Sienna from before dinner is long gone, replaced by this woman who's been hurt by men too many times.

I'm one of them.

So I do the only thing I can do to make her feel safe: I leave.

Blood pounds in my temples as I storm through the house, fists clenching at my sides. Every muscle in my body is coiled tight, rage burning through my veins.

How could I have been so stupid?

I pivot on my heel, pacing the length of the foyer like a caged animal. The cheerful trill of the birds does nothing to soothe my anger. If anything, the sounds of this place only fuel my anger—a constant reminder of the life I've built to get here.

The circus keeps going and going. It never stops.

Not for anyone.

Not even the owner.

Breath rasping in my chest, I run a hand through my hair and tug sharply at the roots. The sting is a welcome distraction from the maelstrom of emotions tearing me apart inside.

Guilt. Regret. Self-loathing.

They war within me, as bright and garish as the lights of the circus. Try as I might, I can't escape the truth. I'm the reason Sienna doesn't trust me.

My mistakes drove her away, and now…

Have I lost her for good?

A shudder runs through me. I can't bear to finish that thought.

Sienna.

The name alone is enough to shatter my fragile composure. My hands curl into fists, nails biting into my palms. If only I could take it all back—rewind to that night and make a different choice. But I can't. My sins are etched into the fabric of time like the gold embroidery on the fortune teller's tent. All I can do now is beg for her forgiveness. Pray that it's not too late.

And take revenge.

Against a woman?

Has it always been leading to this?

Marino would probably laugh if he could see me now.

I stop pacing, chest heaving with each ragged breath. There's no time for self-pity. No time for doubt or inaction. I have to believe there's hope for me and Sienna.

And this time, I won't fail her.

As I stand there, hands clenched at my sides, a familiar voice interrupts my turbulent thoughts.

"Logan?" I glance up to find Liam hovering in the doorway, brow furrowed with concern. Of course he would follow me when I'm like this, distraught.

"I just can't believe it was Alessandra." I drag a hand over my face, impatience simmering beneath my skin. The last thing I need is a discussion about Cirque des Miroirs right now. Not when my mind is consumed with Sienna. "How the fuck was it Alessandra all this time?"

"What is the connection between her and this Kyle Moore?"

Frustration bleeds into my tone as I level a glare at him. "Only Sienna. Kyle was obsessed with her. Thought he would marry her."

Liam stands his ground, jaw set in a stubborn line. "And Alessandra?"

"The only thing she ever cared about was the circus."

"And I'm assuming Sienna was a threat to that."

I meet Liam's gaze, a flicker of hope piercing the darkness that's shrouded me for days. "Now that the circus is back, Alessandra won't be able to stay away."

Liam nods, understanding etched into his expression. "I'll drive."

He drives in silence while I stare out the window, watching the familiar streets of Forrester blur past. My fingers tap an agitated rhythm against my thigh as possibilities swirl through my mind. I've fought to protect Alessandra out of guilt, but that's over now.

Now that she's endangered Sienna.

Why the fuck would she do that? Why would a woman who's been brutalized by men allow that to happen to another woman?

The circus looks the same as it always does: vibrant, half alive.

And waiting.

It's waiting for me to arrive.

I stride through the empty fairgrounds to the fortune teller's tent.

There stands Alessandra in all her eccentric glory—vibrant red hair, colorful kaftan dress, and a knowing smile that makes me wary. "Logan, how wonderful of you to visit. I've been expecting you."

"We have some things to discuss."

Her green eyes glint with secrets, and I have to fight not to demand answers right away. "Indeed we do. Please, come in. You have been busy, but then, so have I."

I enter the dimly lit tent, assaulted by the familiar scents of incense and exotic spices. Alessandra lets the flap fall behind us, then turns to face me, hands clasped.

"Cut the shit, Alessandra. I know you can't actually tell the future."

She smiles. "You never believed. That was your problem."

"Or was your problem that I didn't want to fuck you."

She flinches, caught unaware. "Logan."

I've never really spoken to her like this. I had a soft spot for her because I watched her abuse firsthand, but it turned her into a monster. Or maybe she already was one. Either way, the soft spot has hardened into anger. "Tell me the truth or get the fuck out of here."

"Fine." She pouts. "Ruin the show. You never appreciated it."

I laugh, a harsh sound in the small fortune-telling tent. "I have a great appreciation for the show you put on. It fooled me for a while. Not anymore."

Her lids lower. "You and Cat would have been glorious."

"Cat is a child."

"She's only a few years younger than Sienna."

"More importantly, I knew Cat when she was a child. That's still how I see her. I'm sorry if you thought anything else would happen."

She sits down heavily, landing in the seat the audience uses, near the entrance. Her anger drains away, leaving only exhaustion. "I could have ruled with you, Logan. I wanted to. We would have taken over the world. But when you didn't want me, when it became clear you preferred a younger woman, I thought Cat would be perfect."

"You want an alliance. You want power."

"Yes, damn it. Is that so wrong?"

"No," I say, my voice softer now. "It's not wrong to want power. I know what it was like for you to be powerless. I saw it happen, but you're not going to get it at Cirque des Miroirs."

She draws herself up, struggling to appear haughty. "You wouldn't kick me out."

I stand behind the table where you can see the little cupboard spaces for crystals and other materials. There's an old tarot card deck—the edges softened for authenticity. *Never use a shiny deck,* she told me once. Yes, I have an appreciation for the show now.

The cards feel warm in my hands as I give

them a quick shuffle.

I pull one. The card features a series of cups along with Roman numerals that means eight. In the background, a man walks away.

Alessandra doesn't know it yet, but that man is me.

"What does it mean?"

"The eight of cups means disappointment, abandonment. It means the end."

"Impressive. Maybe you do have a gift of foresight. Because this is the end for you. You're officially leaving. Not temporarily. Not on one of your jaunts. You're gone for good. Cirque des Miroirs no longer has a place for you."

CHAPTER EIGHTEEN

Logan

T HE PHOTO STARES back at me, a permanent reminder of the blood on my hands.

It's from an old newspaper advertisement for the circus my father was in. *Come one, come all. 50 cents to see The Freak Show!* it reads. There's a photo of my father, covered in ink, staring at the camera with dark, dead eyes. I'm looking at it, having found the only quiet space in the fairgrounds. Ironically, it's under the big top, the largest tent.

With no performances happening, it's empty.

Except for me.

Guilt churns in my gut as I gaze into the haunted eyes of the man who fathered me. The circus freak who was hurt by society, so he took out his pain on every woman he found.

Including my mother.

I rake a hand through my hair and sigh. How did we end up here? I started down this path to find myself in him…and ironically, I did. I thought I was saving Alessandra that night. Was I just enabling her? Was I just leading us to this night, where I'd have to send her away?

Was I just becoming the person I fought so hard to resist?

A sideshow. A freak.

A monster.

Shame burns in my chest. I swore I'd never become him, yet one look in the mirror reveals the ugly truth. We share the same ink, the same scars, the same capacity for cruelty.

I bury my head in my hands.

"I'm sorry," I whisper to the ghosts that haunt this place. To the people I've hurt.

To my mother, the first victim of my life, forced to bear me against her will.

To Sienna, because not believing her made me as bad as her bullies.

I'm sorry.

"I accept," Emerson says, breezing into the tent, his expression charming.

Wolfgang is behind him, stone-faced and

severe.

This is happening. Now. Decisions need to be made about Emerson, someone who has been a good friend to me. Someone who saved my life in this very tent.

"Remember how surprised he was?" Wolfgang asks, referencing that long ago night.

They're followed by most members of the circus. The flame thrower. The juggler. The clowns, along with Travis. Even Cat is there, though Alessandra is notably missing.

I stand to face them. "That's about how surprised I feel right now. You coming to host a little coup? Because I have to tell you, it won't be very hard."

The past can't be undone, but the future is still unwritten. I have a chance to do better, to be better. For Cirque des Miroirs. For Sienna.

For myself.

My fingers curl around the edges of the photo as I meet my father's gaze in an old black and white newspaper advertisement. This is where it ends. Today I break the cycle. Today I become the man he always wanted me to be.

The man I was meant to become.

I crumple the old photo, determination steeling my spine.

It's time to face the darkness inside—and finally set it free.

"We're not here to betray you, Logan," Wolfgang says, as if speaking for the group.

It's rare, because usually that's Emerson's role. He's silent as our friend continues.

"We're here to apologize. It may not have been all of us who perpetrated the lie, but it came from us. From the circus. It happened because you trusted us, and we let you down."

I look out over the faces, some of them stoic, some of them attempting smiles, others looking worried. Memories assault me with every breath—the acrid scent of sawdust and sweat, the roar of the crowd, Marino's voice barking orders as animals soared through fire.

This was our kingdom. Now it's my prison.

My fingers brush against the cold metal that holds up the big top, once my sanctuary, now a symbol of all I've lost. I glance up at the billowing canvas overhead, stained crimson and gold by the setting sun. Beauty and blood. The circus's legacy.

"I appreciate the apology. I'm not sure I'm the right leader for you. At least, not anymore."

"You can't give up on us," says someone from the crowd.

I turn to see a mirage of Gerard Marino standing in the center ring, as solid and imposing and fucking cowardly as the day he was overthrown. My heart clenches at the wavery vision of him. *I tried to tell you,* his expression says, icy disappointment etched into his weathered features. *Tried to prepare you for running the circus.*

I take a shuddering breath. *You turned me into a monster.*

The mirage shakes his head. *You've always been a monster.*

His words cut deeper than any knife Wolfgang throws. I squeeze my eyes shut, willing the vision to disappear. When I open them again, he's gone. The space where he once stood is empty. No one hangs from the scaffolding, half naked and whipped… at least not literally. Figuratively I might as well have tied Sienna there myself. The memory of Sienna's face flashes in my mind—the hurt and betrayal in her eyes as I told her to leave. My stomach churns with guilt. I was supposed to protect her, shield her from the violence and shadows of my world.

Instead, I led her straight into the lion's den.

Sienna saw the monster inside me.

She doesn't trust me anymore.

Who could blame her?

"You backed me that night," I say. "It was

unexpected. A pleasant surprise when I expected to die. For that I owe you. I've given you these years, hoping they would be enough."

There's a murmur through the crowd, people commenting on the money, the schedule. The way everything got better. Yeah, I know all of that. To me it didn't seem like a gift I was giving them. It just felt like the way things were supposed to get done.

I look up at the cold metal trapeze, exhaustion and self-loathing threatening to overwhelm me. How did I become this person—cold, manipulative, obsessed with control?

In that moment, I know with stark and sudden clarity that I can't live this way anymore. The cycle of violence ends here. I have to be better than him.

For Sienna's sake… and for my own.

I stand up straighter, steeling my resolve. The first step is facing the damage I've done. Apologizing to Sienna, making things right.

This is my chance at redemption. And I'm not going to waste it.

"Cirque des Miroirs has been my whole world for as long as I can remember. It's been my past even before I started working here, but the future can be anything." Sienna is my future—if she'll have me. I glance around the big top once more, the place that raised and ruined me. "The show is over."

I scrub a hand over my face, haunted by memories. The fear in my mother's face whenever she looked at me. The crack of Gerard Marino's whip on Alessandra.

Cat steps forward, looking like a younger, more innocent version of her mother. "I know we betrayed you, but we're family. You can forgive family, can't you?"

"It's not about forgiveness."

"What is it about then?"

"It's about—" I'm standing here baring my soul to a group of people I've been protecting for years. Even though there's closeness, I've always been separate. First the new guy, the townie. Then the guy who was moving up the ranks too fast. And suddenly, the owner. Most people are intimidated by me. Only Wolfgang and Emerson were ever close. So why the hell am I stripping myself to the bone? Maybe because if I do that they'll know.

They'll know and elect a new leader, as they should.

"It's because I became the monster." A rough laugh. "It's what Marino said that night. That the leader of the circus needed to be callous, needed to be cruel. And I proved him right."

How many times did I swear I'd never become violent?

Yet in the end, I was no better.

Sienna saw that darkness in me. She knew my capacity for violence, had witnessed the beast inside. And still, she loved me.

Against all odds, that girl had cracked through the walls around my heart. She was the first real connection I'd had since my mother died, the only person who could temper the savage impulses bred into me.

With her, the shadows receded. She was light to my darkness, bringing out a side of me I'd long forgotten—the ability to care, to feel, to hope.

I never deserved her. But I was too selfish, too obsessed with possessing her to let her go.

She paid the price for my weakness.

Sienna changed me. Showed me I could be more. And when she left… the light went out. The shadows crept back in, darker than before.

I can't lose her again.

She's out there somewhere, her light calling me home.

And this time, I'm going to claim her.

A surge of adrenaline kicks in as I stride

through the big top, my gaze traveling over the trapezes and platforms suspended high above. This place is in my blood—as much a part of me as the scars that mark my skin. But it's taken enough from me.

I halt in the center of the ring, staring up at the canvas ceiling rippling in the breeze. Gerard Marino built this circus from nothing, devoted his whole life to it… and where did that get him?

Banished from his own circus.

At this point I would almost welcome it.

"I'm sorry," I tell them. "I'm sorry I couldn't be kinder. Or crueler. I'm sorry I couldn't be the owner you need, at least not anymore. Get Wolfgang to do it. Or someone else. I'm done."

There are murmurs, protests, a few people calling out.

Wolfgang looks stoic. Emerson appears almost hurt, which is ironic, because even if I stayed in the circus he wouldn't be allowed here.

A vision of Sienna flashes in my mind, her smile like the sun breaking through storm clouds. My fingers curl into fists.

No. I won't let this place consume me. Not again.

Sienna showed me there's more to life than sawdust and spectacle. I want to wake up without the screams of a crowd in my ears, make a home with the woman I love, start a family… be free of the shadows that dog my every step in this world.

But the Cirque des Miroirs is my legacy. My curse.

Torn between longing for escape and duty to this circus, I stare at the place that made me, wondering if I have the strength to turn my back on everything I've ever known.

A small, fierce flame of hope ignites in my chest.

If finding Sienna means leaving this all behind… then maybe it's time for the circus to end.

Enough. No more living in the past. No more chained to sins that aren't my own.

Today, I choose a different path.

I stand up, spine straight, and take a deep breath. The air tastes clean and full of promise.

It's time to make things right. Protect Sienna. Ensure her safety and happiness, whatever the cost. Even if it means turning my back on the Cirque des Miroirs for good.

I walk into the sunlight, shoulders set, and push it open.

The past is dead. Today, I choose to live.

To love.

CHAPTER NINETEEN

Sienna

TRICKS YIPS AND jumps, chasing after the scrap of fabric I dangle above his head. His paws skid on the sawdust as he tries to catch it, sending up a puff of dust with each slide.

I laugh, the sound bursting from my chest in a way that almost startles me. When was the last time I truly laughed like this?

Maisie laughs, too. "Come on, Tricks! You can do it!"

He finally snatches the fabric from my fingers, shaking his head proudly.

"What a clever boy you are, Tricks!" I ruffle the soft fur between his ears, warmth flooding my chest at his delighted whimpers.

"A prodigy," Maisie announces.

"This scrap of a dog, with his beige fur and curly tail, has brought me more joy than anything else in longer than I can remember."

Her eyes mist. "I'm sad but also happy. Is that weird?"

I smile. "Makes complete sense. That's me all the time these days."

"How are you?" she asks, her voice gentle. "Really?"

"Better, honestly. I mean that. And I want to thank you because you've been a good friend. A true friend, even after I abandoned you."

"You could never," she says.

"I'm serious. If you ever get kidnapped across state lines in a federal offense, you better believe that I'm going to be there on the other side."

She makes a face. "I would just take an espresso as thanks. No one in town can make them now that you're gone."

"Fine, I'll make you an espresso."

"Next time," she says. "I have to help my mom with pies."

The Young family has infamous pies at the county fairs. "Good luck."

As I curl up on the sofa with Tricks, my thoughts drift to the menagerie of animals in the circus. Lions, tigers, bears—all living in cages too small, prodded into performing tricks day after day.

Could I give this lucky dog a better life than that? Take him in, care for him, train him to do simple tricks to delight audiences, all while ensuring he's happy and well-treated?

The dog rests his head on my knee, gazing up at me with liquid brown eyes filled with devotion and trust. My heart clenches. I owe him at least that much, after he risked his life to save mine.

Gently scratching behind his ears, I make a silent promise. This dog will have a home—with me. No more scrambling for scraps, no more shivering in the cold. Just love, warmth, and treats every day.

A smile tugs at my lips as I picture this little fur ball captivating crowds and bringing them the same joy he's brought me. It seems we've both found where we belong.

"What do you say?" I ask the dog softly. "Want to join the circus?"

His enthusiastic bark is all the answer I need.

I dig into my pocket and extract a dog treat, holding it up for the little fur ball to see. His eyes light up, tail wagging in a frenzy of excitement.

"Sit," I command gently.

He immediately plops his rear end on the

ground, gaze fixed on the treat in my hand. I grin and give him the treat, praising him enthusiastically.

"Good boy! What a smart little dog you are." I ruffle the soft fur on his head as he munches on the treat. "Now, lie down."

Again he obeys instantly, belly dropping to the ground as his tail continues to sweep back and forth. Another treat and more praise follows.

We continue like this, me teaching him the simplest of commands and tricks, him performing them with gusto for another treat and a kind word. All the while, warmth and affection bloom inside me like a flower opening to the sun.

Who would have thought, after everything I've endured, I'd find my first real friend in a scruffy little stray dog? Yet here we are. Two castaways who've found where we belong— together.

A lump forms in my throat as I wrap my arms around the dog in a hug. He snuggles into me without hesitation, as if he knows I need this comfort as much as he does.

I close my eyes, breathing in his warm, earthy scent. The arms that hold him are callused and scarred from years of hardship, but for the first time, they embrace with tenderness.

A sharp knock at the front door startles us both. The dog lets out a warning growl as I freeze in place. My heart pounds. Who could it be? Liam and Samantha left on some errand. There are other people in the house—staff, because that's how rich these people are. But I don't know where they are. What if I'm in trouble? What if Kyle got out of jail?

The door creaks open. "Sienna? Are you here?"

My breath whooshes out of me.

"Mom."

She appears, looking so much the same my throat feels tight.

Tricks barks in excitement and my mother jumps back, muttering under her breath.

I hush Tricks and send him into a folded up blanket I've been using as a dog bed.

My mother glances at him nervously as she steps into the room. "I don't like dogs," she says.

"I know, Mom. He is not going to mess with you though, trust me."

After a moment she relaxes and faces me. Her hand reaches out to touch my wrist where there's still faint bruises. "I heard what happened."

I shrug because I don't really know how to discuss it.

I'm not sure what someone in a regular family would do. Maybe the mom would say, *Oh no, it's so terrible something like this happened to you.* And the daughter would be like, *Thank you for caring.*

But the fact is, I got hurt all the time when I lived under her roof and I know she couldn't stop it. She also couldn't stop my father hitting her. But I also know, now that I've had some distance, how it shaped our entire relationship—me and her.

I couldn't trust her to protect me even when I was young.

"They're in jail, you know? Mayor Lindon is talking about the dangers of the circus, how it poisoned their minds."

I roll my eyes. "It wasn't the circus that made them that way. They were already like that."

"Did they…?" She pauses and looks away.

God, this is awkward. And I can guess what she's going to ask. "No," I say, which is technically true, although they got far enough to give me nightmares. But it doesn't matter. I'm not going to tell her that. I'm not going to make her feel bad. Sometimes a lie is what you do to protect the people you love.

She sighs and it hits me, the space between us.

Five feet, almost as if we're strangers.

Her body language doesn't invite closeness. She looks stiff, uncomfortable, almost as if she doesn't want to be there. But the fact is she is here and I'm grateful for that.

I step forward and enfold her in a hug for a moment.

She stands there stiffly and I just breathe in her familiar scent, her shampoo, her perfume and something that's uniquely her. Her hair is always dry. That's what I remember as I press my face against it, the curls springy against my cheek.

Then all at once she releases herself.

Her arms go around me and she hugs me back.

It's a fierce, brief embrace that she breaks away from, as she pats my arm a little harder than necessary.

I hold back a wince.

"You are strong," she says, "but I didn't want this for you."

This. That one word encompasses so much.

A relationship full of violence, a life full of fear.

"You don't have to worry," I say, "they're behind bars. And even if they got out, I am not going to end up with Kyle."

She glances around. "Where is that man?"

My eyebrows lift. "What man?"

"Logan Whitmere."

"He's not here right now but how do you even know his name?"

"He came to the house."

"He came to our house?"

"He was looking for you. He thought I might have something to say that would help find you but I didn't. I have never been able to help you."

A knot forms in my throat. "Well, he did find me. And I'm safe now so you don't have to worry."

"If you need him for money…" She looks around the massive house.

"Oh, this isn't his house. And even if it was, I'm not living here, at least not permanently."

"Will you come home?" she whispers.

My breath catches. Home. Is that what that house was? Not to me. Not ever, really. I always knew it wasn't safe from my earliest memories. "No, Mom," I say, my voice soft, "I'm not coming home."

For a moment, she looks stricken, which takes me by surprise. She's not one to show emotion. Then her face is wiped clear. "Good," she says. "You shouldn't come back. You don't belong in a cabinet."

"In a cabinet?"

She shakes her head. "Will you go back to the circus?"

"I don't know," I say, not because I think I might go back to the circus, but just because I don't know where I'm going. "I'll figure it out."

"You will figure it out with this Logan?"

That one takes me longer to think about. "No, probably not."

"Why not?"

"Because I don't think I can trust him."

She nods without questioning. She knows all about men that can't be trusted. "Then you'll have to find your own path."

"Yeah," I say with an uneven laugh. "I'm still looking for marketable skills. So far serving coffee and telling fake fortunes has been an okay career."

"You are very talented," she says, looking stalwart.

That makes me laugh just because I've never heard her say anything like that before. She isn't someone who particularly gives praise, especially such strong effusive praise like that. "Talented at what?"

"You are talented at making the best of any situation, even bad situations. I've always envied that."

I blink in surprise. "Mom, are you okay? Now that Dad's gone, do you need help?"

She looks embarrassed that I would even ask her that. "No, Sienna, your father left enough for me to live. That is not the issue."

"Then what's the issue?"

She pauses long enough that I think she's not going to answer. Then she says, "The issue is I don't know how to live anymore."

CHAPTER TWENTY

Logan

"WHERE ARE WE going?" she asks.

"It's a surprise," I say, holding her hand as I lead her through a worn-down trail. A squirrel scampers across the path, surprised but unconcerned with our arrival. To the right through the woods, we can see apparatus that the North Security Team members use to train and maintain their physical ability. I gesture toward them. "One day, I'll take you to Nebraska, where the circus' headquarters are. We have our own training center, though most of it is indoors."

"Is being a tough security guard similar to being an acrobat?"

"Easier," I tell her and she laughs. I have my hand linked through hers, and she allows it, something that makes my gut clench because I don't know if she'll still allow it after this outing. I don't know if she should. The truth is, after what she's been through, she deserves a fresh start. She deserves a quaint little one-bedroom apartment somewhere up north probably, where it snows and looks beautiful around the holidays. But damned if I can let her go.

"I feel a little bit like the little girl," she says.

"The one from the show?" The show that's based on Alice in Wonderland. The show I designed to replace the haphazard goofball show that Marino had used for years, a show with an actual storyline to tie all of the acts together.

"Do you know why I picked that one?" I say.

She shakes her head. "A Lewis Carroll fan?"

I chuckle. "Not exactly. I wanted something that involved a little girl, one who didn't necessarily have acrobatic skills. I wanted to give the part to Cat, so that she and Alessandra would be secure in Cirque des Miroirs, so that they would feel safe after…"

"After what?"

"No one ever told you?"

"I heard rumors, nothing specific. I'd rather hear it from you."

"Oh, it's that old cliché story. Boy joins the

circus so that he can feel closer to his terrible father even though he's already passed. Boy discovers the circus is actually pretty decent, but he's new and not that many people trust him. And then, one day he walks in when the owner has decided to punish the resident fortune teller by hanging her upside down in front of everyone and whipping her bloody."

She stops walking, staring at me with her mouth open. "Are you serious?"

"Deadly."

She keeps walking. "So, people said you hooked up with Alessandra after that."

I shake my head wanting her to know the truth even if I never cared about anyone else. "We were never together. Not even once, not even a little bit."

"After the incident, the incident that turned you into the owner, was that a coup?"

"I prefer to call it a hostile takeover."

She gives me a small smile. "So, after you took it over?"

I nod. "Alessandra was nervous about her position in the circus. Understandably, after what had happened, there was some bitterness over the shakeup, over the hostile takeover, and people were angry at her. She wanted to tell people we were together and I allowed it. I wasn't interested in being with anyone else, so it didn't matter to me that they assumed I was taken. If it protected her, then that was fine."

She gives me a sideways glance. "Is that what you did with me?"

"Absolutely not," I say, stopping to face her. "What I did with you was the opposite of protection. It was reckless. It was selfish. I took you into my trailer because I wanted you."

"Oh," she says, her voice faint, her dark lashes hiding her thoughts. Part of me wants to probe, but that's why we're going on this little trip. I take her hand and keep going down the trail. I imagine that hundreds of ex-military men and women have run miles over this particular stretch of ground. They've worn it smooth, with only the occasional tree root lifting up in defiance.

"So I put Cat in the circus so that they would know they had always had a place here and so that everyone else would know that too."

"What was the old owner punishing her for?" That makes me stumble over a tree root, but I catch myself. Yeah, she had to notice the one spot in the story that would make me look like an ass.

"He was punishing her because she was reckless. Because she was impulsive. On one particular night, that night when it was storming, she climbed the Ferris wheel and Emerson nearly cracked his head in half trying to get her down."

"Holy shit," she breathes.

"Yeah," I say, my voice dry. "So that night when they told you, I should have known it was too perfect. It was too close a parallel, but I was caught in the past, like this path we're on that's been worn down smooth, making it easy for people to take it. No rocks and tree trunks in the way, and so once I started down this path, in my mind it just was so easy to keep going, to think that you were like Alessandra, that you had really jeopardized the circus that way. That's what they wanted me to think, and I fell for it."

She's silent as we walk. It's a contemplative silence, a thoughtful one that allows the birds to trill in our wake. Then we've reached the clearing and she gasps. There's a beautiful lake complete with a dock and a rope with multiple knots so you can jump off. There's also—because I came here earlier and prepared it—a picnic blanket.

"Oh, Logan," she says.

I give her a crooked smile. "This is my way of saying I'm sorry, in case that wasn't clear."

She looks at me with haunted, hopeful eyes. "Oh, it's clear."

"Good," I say. "Then don't answer yet. Don't tell me you don't forgive me. Don't tell me you can't be with me. Just spend the day with me here. I have it on good authority that you like to swim in lakes."

"Do you?"

"Someone may have told me that you also like to have grilled cheese sandwiches and soda."

She grins. "Is that what's in the picnic basket?"

"That along with some fruit and a wheel of brie. I think I offended North's chef with my request."

"Good," she says. "I'm starving."

We spend the next few minutes focused on practical matters, where the food will be laid out on level ground, splitting up portions, and then digging into the delicious food. She swallows a bite and then nods toward the lake. "So did you bring me a bathing suit?"

"I did borrow one from Samantha, but I thought if I was very lucky you might go skinny dipping with me."

"Really?" she says drawing out the word, making it unclear which way she's leaning.

"Really," I say, reaching over to tuck her hair behind her ear. My fingers linger against her neck, wanting more contact, more touching. I don't even need sex. Well, that's not strictly true. My cock definitely argues the point. It's always hard when she's around and even harder now that I'm touching her and imagining her naked, but I won't demand sex. Not ever. Not after what she's been through.

She looks away. "I'm not"—she swallows—"You can see with my clothes off, you can tell what happened."

I grit my teeth against the urge to find Kyle in jail and keep punching him until he's gone, until he's off this fucking planet. "That's not your fault. I would never blame you for that. I would never judge you. You're beautiful in every way that you look. You're beautiful no matter what people do to you."

"In that case," she says, "last one in is a rotten egg." And then she stands up. She's tearing off her clothes and I'm distracted.

I'm so fucking distracted by all that beautiful skin, by the curve of her ass, by the bounce of her tits. I'm so distracted that it takes me a minute to even untangle my legs, to stand up, to shove down my jeans and yank off my shirt and then I'm running after her. When we're both running, I realize I can overtake her, but I don't want to.

She's not the rotten one here. And besides back here, I get a wonderful view.

I chase her over to the dock and then she leaps grabbing the rope. She leaps so beautifully, so fearlessly, holding on tight to the rope swing and then letting herself go to flip into the water. I'm right there after her, grabbing it as soon as it swings back to me, I jump and land a few feet away soaking her when she's coming up for air.

God, she looks gorgeous when she's laughing. Courageous, that's what she is. Maybe that's why I believed she could be reckless enough to climb during the storm, but there's one key difference. Alessandra's recklessness came from a place of cruelty. Whether that's justified because of her previous treatment or not, I don't know, but Sienna has never hurt anyone and she never would. The world keeps stepping on her, keeps making excuses.

I pull her close in the water, settling her against my body, letting her rest on me as I kick enough to keep us both afloat. I groan at the feel of her breasts against me.

She holds onto me, one hand on my shoulder, the other drifting down, finding the waistband of my boxer briefs. "Hey. You cheated."

I tug her even closer, breathing the moist air

between us, allowing my mouth to open, my tongue to taste her temple, to lick against her hair. God, I'm starving for her. I couldn't trust myself.

"Sunset, I couldn't trust myself not to slip inside you." She shivers at my words. "But I wanted to be there, nothing between us when I ask your forgiveness or at least the chance of it, when I tell you that I'm sorry."

She leans her forehead against mine. "I know."

"It will take time for me to regain your trust. I know that much, but will you let me try?"

She rocks her head back and forth, almost shaking no, but her forehead stays against mine and I cling to that like a lifeline. Even though we're touching everywhere, my arms wrapped around her beautiful lithe body, her legs wrapped around mine, I still need the connection of our foreheads to feel sane.

"I don't know how this would work," she whispers. "I don't know if I can go back to the circus."

"Forget the circus."

She laughs, disbelieving. "I can't just forget the circus. It's kind of a big deal."

"I'm done with it," I tell her. "I'm not going back."

She pulls away looking shocked. "What do you mean?"

"I already told them. I'm giving it up. They can shut down or they can keep going without me. It's not my problem anymore."

She blinks, looking adorably confused. "You did that. Why? Not for me. It couldn't have been for me."

"Why not?" I demand. "Why aren't you worth giving up the circus? God, you're worth so much more than that."

"You can't give up the circus for me."

"I already have."

She swims away, putting a little distance between us. "I need to think. I mean, this can't be right. It happened so fast."

"The truth is the circus let me down. I had given it so many years of my life for them to do that to you. And in some small way for them to do that to me. It was a betrayal and I won't let them break us up."

She tips her head back, letting it fall into the water, her hair floating around her, almost submerged with only her eyes and nose and beautiful lips still above water. "I don't know where to go from here," she says.

"Will you stay with me, Sunset? Stay with me

as the sun goes down. Stay with me as the orange and purple reflect off your hair. Stay with me until the end of time."

She faces me, solemn. "I want to try," she says. "But I don't know. I need time to think about this. I need time to recover, and the truth is, I need time to consider this new thing about the circus. You always were a package deal. I don't even know who you are without the circus."

The sad truth is I don't know who I am without the circus either, but I'm going to find out. "I'm a man who loves you. That's about the only thing I know for sure right now."

She dives underwater and comes up a few feet away, and the water glistening on her cheeks doesn't only come from the lake. It's tears. I've made her cry.

CHAPTER TWENTY-ONE

Sienna

LOGAN STANDS BEFORE me, his piercing dark eyes filled with anguish, his body strong and dripping wet. "Sienna, I'm so sorry for what I did to you. I was blinded by duty, and I took it out on you."

His words wash over me, a turbulent sea of emotions churning inside. I want nothing more than to melt into his embrace, to forgive him for casting me aside like yesterday's trash. But the scars on my heart remind me that trusting him again would only lead to more pain.

I wrap my arms around myself, steeling my nerves. "Words are empty. How do I know you won't hurt me again? How do I know you won't send me away again?"

"Because I'm not bringing you with me. I'm coming with you." He reaches for my hands, his rough, callused fingers intertwining with mine. "When you left, you took the light from my world. I was in a dark place, Sienna, and you were the only one who could pull me out. I don't ever want to go back to that darkness again."

His touch ignites a spark inside me, fragile and trembling.

Logan brings my hands to his lips, brushing a soft kiss across my knuckles. "You're the best thing that's ever happened to me. I don't deserve your forgiveness, but I'll spend the rest of my life making it up to you. Just give me another chance."

I close my eyes, tears slipping down my cheeks. In my heart, I know Logan is telling the truth. He has always worn his emotions on his sleeve, for better and for worse. If he says that he's changed, then he means it with every fiber of his being.

The walls around my heart start to crumble, brick by brick. I've been so lonely without Logan, adrift on an ocean with no shore in sight. But together, we can weather any storm.

I take a deep breath and open my eyes. The smile that spreads across Logan's face is like the dawn breaking over the horizon, filled with warmth and promise.

"I want to."

Logan's arms wrap around me, enveloping me in his embrace. I cling to him as tears of love spill down my cheeks, the missing piece of my heart finally sliding into place. We have a long road ahead, but as long as we face it together, maybe we can find our way.

His hand comes up to cup my cheek, his thumb brushing away the remnants of my tears. A spark of heat ignites in my core at his touch, the familiar ache of longing blooming to life.

"There's still one more way you can make it up to me," I say, my voice dropping to a husky whisper.

Logan's eyes darken with desire as understanding dawns. "Anything, Sienna. Just name it."

I lean in closer, my lips nearly brushing his. "I need to feel you again. All of you."

A low groan rumbles in Logan's chest. His arms tighten around me, crushing me against him. "Are you sure?" he asks roughly. "I don't want to rush into this if you're not ready."

"I'm ready," I breathe. "We've already wasted too much time apart."

That's all the encouragement Logan needs.

His mouth descends on mine, hungry and demanding. I meet him with equal fervor, desire igniting into an inferno.

Our kisses turn frantic as we shed our clothes, hands roaming over fevered skin. Logan lifts me into his arms and carries me to the grass, laying me down on the bed with reverent care.

"I love you, Sienna," he murmurs, his eyes boring into mine. "Always."

"I love you too," I whisper.

And then there are no more words, only the sweet surrender of two souls and bodies entwining once more.

Our breaths come fast and shallow, mingling in the scant space between us. Logan's hands glide down my sides, leaving a trail of fire in their wake. I arch into his touch with a soft moan.

How did I ever survive without this? Without him?

Logan's lips find the sensitive spot on my neck, teasing the delicate skin there. A riot of sensations assaults me from every direction, overwhelming yet not enough. I need more of him, all of him.

There is no rush, no frenzy. Just unhurried exploration and reverence. Logan worships my body like it's a temple, lavishing attention on every curve and hollow. I do the same, relearning the planes and angles of him through taste and touch.

We know each other's bodies as well as our own, yet it feels new again. A rediscovery. The familiarity is comforting, the novelty exciting.

I gasp as Logan slides into me, stretching and filling me so exquisitely. We lock eyes, azure meeting obsidian, and for a moment we stay still, suspended in the perfection of the moment.

Then we move as one, a dance in the water borne of intimacy and trust. Each caress, each thrust builds the fire within me, stoking it higher and higher until I'm engulfed in flames. The water is cool against my skin, but nothing can fight the fire.

Logan quickens his pace, chasing his own release, and I tumble over the edge into mindless ecstasy. He follows soon after, my name a ragged cry on his lips.

We cling to each other as the tremors subside, hearts pounding out a syncopated rhythm. No words are needed in this perfect silence.

Just two souls weaved as one. Whole once more.

The surface of the lake ripples around us, as if we're the epicenter of the universe.

In this moment, we are.

I nestle closer into Logan's embrace, savoring the warmth and solidness of him. His arms tighten around me in response, as if he can't get enough of this closeness either.

We have a long road ahead to rebuild what we once had, but in this moment I have no doubts that we'll make it. That we'll come out the other side stronger and better than before.

Logan brushes a kiss against my hair, his breath stirring the strands. "I'm sorry for breaking your trust in me. I was a fool to ever let you go." His voice is rough with emotion. "I don't deserve another chance, but I'm going to spend the rest of my life making it up to you. Loving you the way you deserve."

I tilt my head up to meet his gaze. "I wouldn't have let you back in if I didn't think you were worthy of forgiveness." I cup his cheek, rubbing my thumb over the sharp angle of his cheekbone. "We both made mistakes. But we've been given an opportunity for a fresh start. A chance to build something better and more lasting."

"A chance I don't intend to waste." Logan seals his vow with a searing kiss that steals my breath.

When we part, I see nothing but truth and

longing in the depths of his eyes. The fears and doubts that once plagued me melt away under the intensity of his gaze.

"I love you," I say simply.

A brilliant smile curves Logan's lips. "And I love you, Sunset."

Logan's hands blaze a trail of fire over my skin as our bodies move together in a rhythm as old as time. Each touch, each caress is an act of worship—a prayer for forgiveness and a promise for the future.

Our breaths come in ragged gasps, the air redolent with the scent of sweat and sex. But beneath the hunger and desire simmers a deeper connection—a bond forged through heartbreak and tempered by time.

"Look at me," Logan rasps, his eyes burning into mine. I meet his gaze unflinchingly, no barriers left between us.

In the depths of his eyes, I see the truth—that the past can never be erased, but it can be forgiven. That love, when given another chance, can emerge stronger and more resilient.

A cry spills from my lips as pleasure washes over me in waves, blotting out everything but the feel of Logan surrounding me, anchoring me in the here and now.

Logan follows soon after, his face buried in the curve of my neck as he whispers my name like a benediction.

We hold onto each other as our heartbeats slow, reluctant to let go now that we've found our way back into each other's arms.

The air is filled with the scent of our desire, the air heavy with the intoxicating mix of sweat and longing, as we surrender to the moment and to each other.

Time seems to stand still as we reach the pinnacle of our passion, our bodies trembling with release and our hearts finally finding solace in each other's embrace.

The world narrows to just the two of us, cocooned in our own little bubble of bliss. The steady beat of Logan's heart against my cheek grounds me, chasing away the last vestiges of doubt and fear.

Here, in Logan's arms, is where I belong.

Here, with Logan, is home.

A lump forms in my throat, emotions welling up inside me. I cling to him, afraid that if I let go, this will all turn out to be just another dream.

Logan tightens his hold on me as he walks us back out of the water, and I can feel the tension seep from his body. We have a long road ahead of us, strewn with obstacles and past hurts that we must work through. But as long as we stand together, side by side and heart to heart, we can overcome them all.

As we lie tangled in each other's arms, our breathing slowly returning to normal, a sense of peace washes over me. It brings with it a glimmer of hope for a future filled with love and redemption.

CHAPTER TWENTY-TWO

Sienna

IN THE SUNLIT sitting room I guide Tricks through a repertoire that includes spins, jumps, walking on a very thin piece of wood forward and then backward, and barking on command. I'm not sure what we're leading up to, precisely. But he enjoys the challenge, as well as the treats that come afterward. And I enjoy the sense of purpose.

Samantha plays violin one room upstairs, something with a slightly playful, jaunty sound that perfectly suits Tricks. Along with a faint haunting note that suits me.

The notes waft down the spiral staircase.

Logan came back exhausted late last night. I wanted to talk to him about it, but he pressed between my knees and made me come so hard I couldn't speak. Perhaps that was on purpose. He went back today to handle some "housekeeping," as he called it. Though perhaps the term *cleaning out his desk* would be more appropriate. If instead of a desk it was an entire circus with all its tents and its trucks and its secrets.

Men with military bearings walk through the house for important, top-secret security briefings with Liam North in his office. The contrast between the refined music and the severity of their bearings tickles me. It reminds me of the circus with its fluid acrobats and high level of pomp.

One man stops to watch as I attempt to teach Tricks how to cover his eyes with his paws while he's lying down. He's fine with piling his paws on his snoot but struggles to understand actually closing his eyes and covering them.

"*Yes*," I say when one paw nudges higher. "That's exactly right, Tricks."

Naturally he gets a cheese cube.

"Impressive," comes a lower voice from the hallway, and I whirl to see a tall, handsome man with blond hair and blue eyes. He looks like a real-life version of Captain America.

I manage a smile. "Yeah, well, sometimes the world is too much. We have to be able to close our eyes to catch a break."

He grins, taking a step deeper into the room. Tricks cocks his head at him, as if more curious than concerned about the approaching stranger. "The world can be a dark place," he agrees. "Though rather than closing my eyes, I prefer to look at beautiful things…and people. Like you."

My cheeks feel warm. "Nice line."

"Thanks, I workshopped it in my head for one point five seconds."

That surprises a laugh out of me. "Aren't you supposed to be working?"

He holds out his hand. "Jason Malone. And yes, but I couldn't resist the show."

I shake his hand, feeling a little shy. "Sienna Cole."

"You with the circus?"

It's on the tip of my tongue to say no, to refute the connection, to refuse the memories. Except that wouldn't be true, would it? It wouldn't be honest. Whatever my feelings about Cirque des Miroirs, they offered me a chance to escape. They also booted me out. It's a complex relationship…but it *is* a relationship. "Yes."

He nods. "Thought so. After all, you've got a lion tamed."

Tricks wags his curved little tail, clearly enamored with the praise. I can't say that I mind it, either. I give a small performance bow. "That's me. A lion tamer."

"Maybe I'll see you around, Sienna of the Circus." He winks before heading deeper into the house, clearly running some important errands for Liam. Probably state secrets.

I look down at Tricks. "Are you really tamed or is it an act?

He pants cheerfully in answer.

And it occurs to me that we could create a routine out of these tricks.

That we could set it to the beat of the music.

That we could turn it into a story.

Tricks looks up at me, his one-ear-up-one-ear-down stance ready, brown eyes focused on me, absorbing my cues. I give a slight gesture that means for him to stand up on his back legs. Which he does. I stand a little straighter, showing him the grace I want from my furry student. And then I cross one foot in front of the other.

He mirrors me, holding his balance.

I start with simple commands, letting the music guide me.

Professional musicians must have to practice the same piece over and over again. Which makes the perfect backdrop for me to choreograph this routine. We progress to his more complex tricks: weaving through my legs, jumping through a hoop, and even bowing at the end in perfect harmony with me. My determination, his enthusiasm. We move together fluidly, executing spins, twirls, and leaps. It takes coordination.

It takes teamwork.

Tricks is perfectly attuned to me.

Our bond is built on trust and mutual understanding. Mutual respect.

When we're done I roll onto the ground with a laugh of delight, letting him stand on top of me as I scratch behind his neck. "What a good boy. What an incredible boy."

The sound of clapping shakes me out of my joyous reverie.

I sit up, surprised to find Travis. "What are you doing here?"

He gestures toward the front door. "We brought Logan's RV."

Dread coils in my stomach. Part of me thought he wouldn't really do it. It's a testament of his devotion to me, of course. A requirement of his penance, I suppose. But it feels wrong. He belongs in the circus. And the circus belongs in him. "I see."

"Everything's in an uproar. No one knows

what's going to happen next. We might shut down."

I lift one eyebrow at him. I might have had the same worry, but I'm not interested in letting Travis see my doubt. "Do you want me to do something about it?"

"You could convince him to come back."

"Why would I do that?"

He flushes, always such a bright red on his pale face. No wonder he likes the heavy paint makeup that clowns use. It truly masks him in a way he could never do in real life. "Because we need him. You know we do. We don't fit in anywhere else."

"Then you should have thought of that before you lied to him."

"I wasn't part of that," he says, a little fast, a little too defensively.

"Weren't you?"

"Look, I'm sorry that I backed away from you, from our friendship. You know how bad it was with Kyle. You saw most of it when you were trying to protect me."

A sigh escapes me, washing away some of my righteous indignation. "I was trying to protect you. Logan was trying to protect Alessandra. In a way we succeeded all this time, but at what cost?

Ourselves, that's what."

He flinches. "I'm sorry, okay? I'm sorry. What else can I say?"

"Nothing. You don't need to say anything, because I forgive you. But I can't do it anymore, the same way Logan can't give himself up for the circus. We won't be martyrs anymore."

"You were never a martyr to me."

"No? You let me take punches for you, but you wouldn't even talk to me at lunch. What the hell does that make me? You may have consoled yourself that you weren't the one to actually hit me, but turning away from me as a human hurt even worse than the physical pain."

Confusion. Then a quiet realization. "You've changed."

I nod. "Thank God for that."

"You were always so tough. I wanted to be like that."

"I'm tired of being tough. I want to live in peace. If that means walking away from the people who were supposed to love me, supposed to protect me, then that's what I'll do."

"So you'll let him walk away from Cirque des Miroirs?"

"You can have the circus. I have Logan." And something else. A deep sense of self-worth. I don't really blame Travis for being afraid, for acting out in trauma. That is his journey to walk. I've been walking my own tumultuous, rocky version. And I've finally found a clearing with a lake and a picnic basket. And a man who chooses that clearing over everything else.

He's leaving the circus for good.

It feels like confirmation, like absolution.

It also feels wrong.

Three men walk through the door leaving boxes inside. Logan's stuff.

They pause when they see me. Two of them look guilty. The third looks pissed.

"You're the one making him leave," he says.

I shake my head. "He's a grown man who makes his own choices."

The man takes a step forward, slightly menacing. "And what about us? He's taking away our choices. You're doing it, by letting him leave for you."

Fear ruffles my stomach. The hair on the back of Trick's back rises. He stands between me and them, growling, looking ready to bite them.

Booted steps approach. Then someone appears. The man from earlier. Jason Malone. "There a problem?" he asks, his voice deceptively soft.

"They were just leaving," I say, my voice strong. Confident. I know where I belong now. I know what I'm worth. And I don't need to answer to these men who are strong in numbers but weak alone. Who would make a woman feel scared to be in a room with them.

"Then get," Malone says with the same softly menacing voice.

They scramble to leave.

I watch as Travis and the other circus clowns drive away, the dog at my side.

He yips at me, and I reach down to scratch his ears with a misted smile. "Thanks, Tricks. And thank you, Jason. I appreciate the assist."

Jason nods, his expression grim. "Let me know if you need anything. Seriously."

"Thank you." This is what Logan meant when he said I don't have to do it alone. That society was supposed to protect me, because I'm not a six-foot-tall god with muscles for days. I can't always protect myself, but that's not weakness.

Weakness would be letting them keep me from living my life.

It makes me wonder about the circus.

It makes me wonder whether some of my assumptions were wrong.

When Logan makes it back that night, looking tired but resolved, I throw my arms around him. "Missed you."

"I heard what happened."

"Oh, they shouldn't have bothered you with that. It was fine."

"They shouldn't have approached you."

"I know, but Jason was there."

His arms go around my waist, tugging me flush against his muscled body. "Jason, huh?"

"You jealous?" I ask, mostly teasing.

"Maybe," he says, his voice gruff. "It doesn't escape me that you could have someone like him."

"Like him how?"

"You know, someone without tattoos. Someone without baggage."

That makes me smile. "Pretty sure military dudes have tattoos, too. And baggage."

"Fine. Someone without a circus."

"That's what you are now, though. Isn't it?"

"Yeah," he says, voice rough. "That's what I am now."

I reach up a hand to cup his jaw. "Are you okay?"

"I'm always okay when I have you in my arms."

That sounds suspiciously like a *no*. "What's this?" I ask, feeling something in his back pocket.

He pulls it around, and I watch a succession of emotions cross his darkly handsome face: grief, frustration, gratitude. He opens it, revealing several bundles of faded red triangular cloth, along with a tattered streamer that reads CIRQUE DES MIROIRS. "They fly at the top of the tents."

I blink. "What will they use now?"

"It's tradition." A rough laugh. "The circus loves its traditions. They replace them every year. And at the end of every season, the owner of the circus gifts these to someone who made a big impact."

My heart clenches. "Oh, Logan."

"I didn't plan to take them. Wolfgang forced them on me."

I swallow hard against the lump in my throat. "I don't know if I can let you do this, Logan. If I can let you give up the circus for me."

He cups my face gently, gazing at me with a tenderness that makes my chest ache. "Don't say that, Sunset. You're mine. I'm yours."

I close my eyes, leaning into his touch. How is it that after everything, he still knows exactly what to say to reach into my heart?

"We belong together, Sienna. Through all the ups and downs, all the challenges we face, we will get through them together. Because what we have is bigger than any obstacle. Our love can overcome anything."

A single tear slips down my cheek as my remaining doubts and fears begin to crumble. He's right. Our love is bigger than any challenge. And it's time I stopped running from it.

He bends down to kiss me, first with soft nips of his lips, then with deeper explorations that leave me breathless. It's the middle of the day, but that doesn't stop him from lifting me in his arms and carrying me upstairs to the bedroom. I don't think he cares who sees us. No, that's not true. I think he *wants* Jason Malone and whoever else is here to see.

The possessiveness makes me turn liquid between my legs.

He spends the next few hours playing in that space, licking and touching.

Making love to me until I'm moaning into the pillow.

Maybe he does want the whole house to hear me, because he doesn't let up.

Only later that night, when I'm looking up at the moonlight, do I have time to think.

I don't give a shit about what the clowns do without their owner to guide them. That's not my concern. But it *is* my concern what Logan

Whitmere needs.

The truth is I don't want a man who's un-complicated.

One who's black and white.

I want the shadows.

And the light.

The sunlight dappled through trees, forming gruesome faces on my skin, the way I saw in my treehouse the day I first heard about Cirque des Miroirs coming to town.

I want someone who lives in those liminal spaces.

And even though he's willing to give up the circus for me, that won't be what makes him happy.

Maybe there's a way that we can have both.

Maybe we don't have to give up things that bring us joy just to be safe.

CHAPTER TWENTY-THREE

Sienna

I DON'T HAVE a car or my bicycle from home. Logan would take me anywhere—probably even Paris, if I asked—but he'd have feelings about this particular field trip. I could probably ask Liam and Samantha for a ride, but no doubt that would come with personal security. I'm all for safety after my last road trip, which took place in a trunk, but in this case it would count as intimidation. So when I get the text from Maisie about the county fair, I call in unlikely reinforcements. My mother.

The irony is that we're in my father's truck.

It was a symbol of her isolation, before. That he could leave, and she couldn't. Now it's the path to her freedom, even if she doesn't yet know where it should take her.

At first glance the Forrester County Fair looks like a cheerful place: colorful bunting, the aroma of caramelized popcorn lingering in the air, and the distant laughter of children.

Beneath the façade of civility lurks an unsettling air, a sense of unease that only grows as more people notice me and my mother. Whispers work their way through the bustling crowd. The same people who looked at us in disdain now see us with…fear.

They know that I'm with a powerful man, a strong man, a dangerous man.

One who can beat up the town's bullies and send them to jail.

I don't want their fear, but I've come to realize there is no other option for some people.

They don't see me as human.

They don't see me as one of them, so they can only look down on me or fear me.

Regular human respect, somehow, isn't even an option.

The carousel here is about two decades older than the one at Cirque des Miroirs—and maintained worse, too. The cheerful music has split seconds of jarring silence. The flashing lights seem manic. The antique horses freeze in macabre expressions, their painted eyes following passersby with an eerie intensity.

Some children shake their heads when offered a ride.

No, thank you.

We walk through the grounds, passing the rows of livestock that will be judged.

Our destination is the market area, where booths are setup to sell fresh fruit, local honey, and jerky. The folded tables are covered with white plastic tablecloths that whip in the wind.

She doesn't have a fancy sign or even a costume.

Instead the fortune teller wears a cropped T-shirt and jeans.

In her hands she holds worn-looking tarot cards.

There appear to be no takers at the moment, so I leave my mother at a stand selling homemade jewelry and walk up to the booth.

"Hello, Cat."

She doesn't look surprised to see me. "Want your fortune told? Ten dollars to pull a card. The mystic world has the answers you're seeking."

"Is this your new thing?"

"Maybe. I'm trying it out. I need to find something new since I can't stay at the Cirque des

Miroirs anymore."

"Is it shutting down, then? I wasn't sure."

"I don't know. Maybe. Wolfgang is the only person who could do it, and he doesn't want to. My mother is talking about stepping in, trying to form a quorum, as she calls it." Cat rolls her eyes. "She's always been obsessed with ruling the circus. She sees this as her chance."

"Oh." The news makes me sad. Not because I don't want Alessandra to lead, but because I already know she can't. What Logan did with them was singular. It takes strength to lead. True strength, the kind that isn't based on fear and greed and grasping.

"I know," Cat says, her voice dry.

My eyebrows raise. "I thought you lied about the Ferris wheel to help her."

She runs a hand over her face. "I lied about it to impress Emerson, which didn't even work. It only resulted in making him look at me as some malleable child."

"That sucks."

"Don't lie. That's what I deserve."

A surprised laugh escapes me. "Maybe."

"Definitely. I was a cunt. And I'm sorry. Truly."

Her apology rings true. Truer than Travis's

defensive words, anyway. "I didn't know you even wanted to be a fortune teller."

"I didn't. It was always my mom's thing, but it's something I know how to do." She makes a face. "I know it's hard to believe, but we actually have the whole *second sight* thing."

"Wait. Really? I thought it was part of the show."

"We have visions. Whatever. They aren't useful in the slightest."

"You can tell the future but it's not useful?'

"We get these glimpses, but they're just one possible outcome. I saw you ruling the circus, but then we interfered and ruined it. When ironically, you could have made it better."

"I thought a vision would have shown me destroying it."

"It doesn't matter. The visions don't matter. All that matters is our choices."

Yes. Our choices. Something about that nags me, but I'm struck by the tarot cards in her hands. Maybe I'm gullible, and all she wants is ten dollars. Something compels me to pull out a ten dollar bill and lay it on the table.

Her eyebrows raise, but she doesn't question it. She slips the money into her pocket and splits the deck. Then she pulls a card. It's one I've never actually pulled for someone else. Only seen it when I was reading about it online or shuffling through the deck.

The High Priestess.

The card pictures a woman with flowing robes holding an ancient scroll, wearing an illuminated crown on her head.

Her eyes narrow. "She represents divine knowledge. Is your intuition trying to tell you something?"

That strikes a chord inside me, one that resonates past me into Logan, into the wider world and our impact on it. I give her a rueful smile. "Is that your way of trying to convince me to make Logan go back to Cirque des Miroirs? Travis already tried that."

She snorts. "There's more likely going to be a place for it if my mom takes it over than if Logan comes back. He won't let me within twelve inches of you. I'm surprised you're even here without him."

"He doesn't precisely know I'm gone."

"I'll always have a soft place for the circus, and for Logan, for giving me a part in the show so early. But I realized when it ended that I'd been limiting myself. I fixated on Emerson because he was handsome and available in the circus, instead of because I truly loved him. I need to explore more of the world, without my mother's influence, without Logan's protection, before I know what I really want."

I nod, understanding the inclination. Some people try to harm us. Others try to help. But in the end only we can know where we're going in this life. And who we want to become. "You know, I think in a different life we could have been friends."

She shakes her head, which feels like an indictment of herself. "Maybe in another life we will be."

I suppose I could hold a grudge, but that feels pointless. Maisie was a true friend. Travis wasn't. Maybe Cat can be something else…a friendship that grows. "I'd like that."

I find my mother at another table, this one laden with handmade wood carvings. They're shaped like woodland symbols: squirrels, mushrooms, the occasional gnome.

"I could do this," she says without looking up from a sculpture of a mama fox and baby fox.

"You mean carve wood?"

"I could create dolls with the batik fabric I have stored away." She looks up, her expression uncertain. She looks different than she did for most of my life. Less distant. Out of the trance of survival. More human. "And then maybe sell them at fairs?"

Or on Etsy. I have no idea what the market is like for hand-crafted dolls, but that's not important. What matters is that she feels like she can live again. "I think it's a great idea, Mom. If there's any way that I can help you, I will."

She pats my cheek. "No."

That one word. No. It isn't a rebuff. It's a statement of identity. Of purpose. Because finding our purpose isn't only for the young. It's for every age. Each day we decide who we'll be. Pride warms my chest as I watch her study their signs with pricing, deals, and newsletter signups. She's already studying the business aspect.

Every day is a new beginning.

Every day is the start of a brand-new show.

CHAPTER TWENTY-FOUR

Sienna

"WHERE ARE WE going?" Logan asks.

"I'm allowed to have surprises, too," I tell him with a serene smile. Wolfgang is driving us down one of the country roads in the SUV. Little Tricks is trying to shove his nose into my pocket where I have some tiny cheese cubes stored. Even through a plastic bag, he can smell them. And he's ready to do any number of tricks—or thievery—to get it.

Logan's breath catches when he sees the spires of the circus, the red flags noticeably missing from the tops. He holds my hand. "Sienna. What are we doing here?"

I stare up into his piercing blue eyes, searching for any hint of deception. But all I see is sincerity.

Raw pain and longing that mirror my own.

How can I turn him away when he's baring his soul to me like this?

When all I've wanted is to live in the joy of the circus again?

His joy. My peace.

We deserve them both.

"You're not leaving the circus."

"Yes, I am," he says, his voice a low growl.

"No, you're not. And I'm not running away with the circus this time. I'm running away with you."

"No," he breathes. "The circus hurt you. *I* hurt you."

A wry twist of my lips. "Families do that sometimes. And isn't that what you told me? The circus means family. Bring me with you, Logan."

"Sienna."

"Call me *Sunset*."

"Sunset. You don't need to do this for me."

"Then let me do it for me. I have this idea." The SUV pulls to a stop in front of the fairgrounds, and I step out with Tricks at my side. I spread my arms wide. "Introducing the fabulously talented, compact-sized new show, Little Tricks!"

A smile spreads across his face. "And you?"

"And me."

"You want to stand under the big top, to delight the crowds with your smile?"

"If you'll have me. You're still the circus owner, last I checked."

"Oh God. Yes, Sunset. Run away with me."

His lips find mine, and I melt into his embrace. Our past may be scarred, but the future is ours to write. Together.

My heart swells as Logan holds me close, his warmth seeping into my skin. For the first time since we were reunited, I feel at peace. Like I can finally breathe again.

I pull back to meet his gaze, seeing nothing but love and sincerity in his eyes. "I'm tired of running, Logan. I don't want to spend my life looking over my shoulder, waiting for the other shoe to drop. I want to stop surviving and start living again."

He brushes his thumb over my cheek, his smile softening. "Live this life we're meant to share together. The circus will be yours. My gift to you."

"It's not easy," I whisper. "Letting go of the past, learning to trust again. There will always be moments of doubt, when those old fears and insecurities come creeping back in."

"I know." His hand slides down to clasp

mine, gripping it firmly. "We all have our doubts and fears. God knows I have plenty of my own. But we have to believe that this love we share is strong enough to overcome them."

I cling to his hand, drawing strength from his touch. "I want to believe that. I want a future with you, without the darkness of our past haunting me."

"You can have that future." He pulls me into his arms again, resting his chin atop my head. "The past is behind us. This is a new beginning, a chance to build the life we always dreamed of. As long as we're together, we can get through anything."

I close my eyes and breathe him in, feeling the last of my doubts fade away. He's right about it all—about everything. The past is behind us, and the future is ours to shape.

Our story may have had a rocky start, but we get to decide how it ends. And this is one story that will have a happy ending after all.

He brushes a kiss over my forehead. "You deserve to be happy."

I pull him down for a proper kiss, sighing against his lips. "So do you. I'm sorry for doubting you."

"Don't be." His arms tighten around me.

"You had every reason to doubt me. I'm the one who should be sorry for breaking your trust in the first place."

"The past is behind us now."

"You're right." He kisses me again, slow and sweet. "We were meant to be, you and I. Nothing can tear us apart now."

I lead him into the big top, which is empty except for a small pedestal painted white with red triangles pointing down, like the flags that are on top of the tents.

"Let's show him what you can do, Tricks."

We flow through the routine we've been practicing. Everything flows perfectly. Tricks hits every moment with the perfect amount of timing and personality.

Tricks's hopeful expression when he's done makes Logan laugh.

"It's the end," he says.

I blink. "The act?"

"It's the perfect ending. Especially with the little girl who goes through Wonderland, that confusing and wondrous place. She brings magic back home with her. She may return to the regular world, but everything she's seen and experienced, it's changed her."

"Yes." My eyes mist. "That's right."

"She's you," he murmurs, stepping close.

"What do you mean?"

"You're that little girl, but you're also the magic."

"I don't understand." Except maybe I do.

He holds me in a warm embrace. "Can't you see, sunset? You're my grand finale."

"And you, Logan, are my home."

I lean back and whisper, "I taught Tricks something else."

"What's that?"

"Privacy, Tricks."

He lies down and covers his face with his little paws.

Logan's laugh drives away the shadows.

The steady beat of his heart against mine is soothing, chasing away the last vestiges of doubt and fear. Our path won't always be easy, but together we can overcome any challenge. The future is ours, and this time, I'm ready to embrace it without looking back.

I nestle closer against Logan's warmth, content in the silence. There's no need for words between us, not when we can communicate so much through a single touch or glance.

After a while, Logan speaks again, his voice soft. "I know I've hurt you in the past, Sienna, and I can't take that back. But I want you to know that I'm committed to making things right. You're the best thing that's ever happened to me, and I don't intend to lose you again."

His words melt the last of my doubts, like the sun breaking through clouds. I lift my head to meet his gaze, a smile curving my lips. "I believe you."

Logan's eyes widen, as if he can scarcely dare to hope. "You do?"

"Yes." I brush my fingers along his jaw, rough with stubble. "The Logan I knew before would never have fought so hard for us or bared his soul the way you did. You've changed, and I can see now how much I truly mean to you."

A slow smile spreads across his face, brighter than any spotlight. "You mean everything to me, Sienna. My life, my heart, my soul—they all belong to you."

Joy swells within me, overflowing in a laugh. I throw my arms around his neck, clinging to him as he spins me in circles. Leaving only love and trust in their wake.

Tricks barks and spins in circles, excited by the prospect of cheese—and our joy.

We've endured loss and heartbreak, faced impossible odds, but our love has endured.

Stronger than any storm or trial, vast and deep as the ocean—endless as the horizon.

After all we've survived, I know that this love will last forever.

Logan sets me back on my feet, cupping my face in his hands. His eyes gleam with equal parts passion and tenderness. "Run away with the circus. Not just for a short time. Forever. Be my partner in all things—in ruling the circus, in life, in love. Stay by my side always, as I will stay by yours, and build a future together."

Joy and longing surge through me in a wave. "Yes. A thousand times, yes."

His answering smile is like the sun breaking over the horizon, warm and bright. He kisses me then, a sweet and searching kiss that steals my breath away.

When we break apart, I'm dizzy with love and desire.

His hands roam over me, igniting fires beneath my skin, as our kisses grow increasingly heated and urgent.

I cling to him, drowning in sensation, losing myself in his embrace. Our clothing falls away, baring flesh to seeking hands and hungry mouths.

Logan enters me in a smooth thrust, and I gasp at the familiar ache and fullness. We move together, a dance as old as time, building toward a climax that will shake me to the core.

His eyes lock with mine, blue as the deepest ocean and fathomless. "I love you, Sienna. Today, tomorrow and forever."

"And I love you," I breathe.

Our rhythm accelerates, pleasure coiling tighter and tighter within me. At last it crests and breaks, a wave of ecstasy that leaves me trembling and crying out his name.

Logan follows after, his face buried in my neck as he groans his release. We cling to each other, hearts pounding as one, basking in the warmth and joy of our union.

The circus has always been his home, but in this moment I realize that it's truly mine as well. Because this is where we belong—in each other's arms, where we've found our heart's true home.

The sudden shouting outside the big top shatters our peaceful afterglow. Logan frowns, disentangling from my embrace and grabbing his discarded pants.

Logan yanks on his shirt and strides to the door, flinging open the flap—then freezes in shock. Two police officers stand outside, their expressions grim.

My heart leaps into my throat as a chill races

down my spine. This can't be good.

"Logan Whitmere, you're under arrest for murder."

Oh God. No.

But the officers are already grabbing Logan's arms, snapping handcuffs over his wrists as they recite his rights. He doesn't resist, merely throwing a glance over his shoulder at me. His eyes are calm and steady, filled with determination.

Don't worry, that look seems to say. *I'll fix this.*

I can only stare at him mutely, my mind reeling. Murder? That's serious. Especially in Texas. Death penalty serious. Did Kyle die from his injuries?

"That was self-defense," I say, trying to stand in their way. "Everyone saw."

They push past me as if I'm nothing. "This isn't about Kyle. It's about a woman named Alessandra Gallo. She turned up dead this morning."

Oh God.

As the police lead Logan away, he calls back to me in a strong, grim tone. "Call Liam. Don't say anything. To anyone."

The officers haul him off before I can respond, leaving me alone and adrift in a sea of confusion and dismay. My fingers curl into fists, nails biting into my palms. Alone. I'm alone again. What if there's no way out of this for Logan?

I already know he killed my father. What if he's actually guilty?

Thank you for reading WHITE LIES! The stunning conclusion to the Cirque des Miroirs trilogy is BLACK SHEEP, which comes out soon.

In the meantime, you can get Liam and Samantha's forbidden romance, OVERTURE, for free right now.

You can also order ringmaster Emerson Durand's story, BLUE MOON …

Charismatic. Devious. Secretive. Emerson Durand is the ringmaster for the illustrious Cirque des Miroirs. In each city he finds a new woman to command for the night. Until he finds the one woman who doesn't bow to his demands.

Luna Rider soars through the air as an aerial acrobat. She's determined to provide for herself and her sister, but she doesn't count on being gambled away. Or the secrets that hover under the striped tent.

Turn the page to read a steamy excerpt from the book…

Excerpt from Blue Moon

Luna

M Y HEART SLOWS down in the moments before a performance.

Every second seems to last an hour.

I feel the energy coming off the crowd as they clap and stomp for the tiger who's performing on stage right now. I've seen the same act so many times, so many years of my life that even from backstage, I can see him in my mind standing on his hind feet.

I can see him bouncing a ball.

I can see him jumping through a hoop lit on fire.

There's still a patch of rough skin on his left paw where it caught once during a performance. I can still smell the singed fur and hear the screams of people in the audience.

That won't happen tonight because for the most part, we don't make mistakes.

It's not really professional pride or pleasure at

the audience's delight that drives us.

It's my father. He's cruel, merciless.

Mistakes get eliminated, which means they end up rolled into a river somewhere between one town and another as the circus moves along.

So we all learn to do our parts, to play them well.

We learn to smile so hard that no one in the audience ever guesses that we're terrified.

I lean down to stretch my hamstrings, forcing my nose all the way between my legs. When I go out there I need to be limber. But we still have five minutes.

Every drum from the band, every gasp from the audience, they're all choreographed.

They're all a familiar countdown.

One I've played night after night for most of my life.

Maybe for some people the circus is a job.

I've heard distantly that it can even be a dream.

For me, it's only ever been duty.

Duty that I was raised to perform since I was a baby. As a toddler my father taught me to walk on a tightrope. He put down padding when he taught me, but only because bruises are not conducive to performances. I still got them though, bruises. I fell so many times that the bruises started forming on my feet. My skin would crack open and my father would pick me back up and put me on the tightrope even as blood dripped down onto the mats. That's how I learned balance.

After stretching forward, I stand up straight and then lean backwards and backwards and backwards. Flexibility. Sometimes people come up to me after a show and marvel over how my body is so flexible. Am I double-jointed? they ask. Was I just built this way? No. My body started off like everyone else's, but I pushed harder than I should have, harder than is safe, and even then my father stepped in and pushed harder.

Flexibility was the only way that I could escape the injury he inflicted on me.

So I learned it.

Standing with my feet planted firmly on the ground, I bend backwards until I can reach my ankles, then I come back up again and freeze because someone is there—a man.

He has dark hair, a little glossy with a surprising amount of volume.

One part falls rakishly over his eye.

Dashing, that's the word that comes to mind.

He looks dashing.

Which I distrust immediately.

Dashing isn't real, it's a fairy tale.

And I learned a long time ago that fairy tales don't exist.

The twinkle of mischief in his eyes proves me right. The fact that he's tall with broad shoulders, obviously strong, even through his suit, that doesn't matter. None of it matters.

He's a stranger and even worse, a townie.

Circus folk are insular, almost xenophobic.

We take money from the people in town. We serve them popcorn and we perform for them, but we never trust them. He is some member of the audience who decided to sneak backstage for reasons unknown. Probably so he could hit on the performers.

It'll be a lucky thing if my father doesn't see him.

Underperforming circus folk aren't the only people he's ever rolled into a ditch as the caravan moved through a lone moonlit highway.

The man leans back against a temporary wooden wall.

"Like what you see?" he asks.

My cheeks flush, I've been staring like an idiot. "You shouldn't be back here."

He looks around. "I don't see a sign."

"There doesn't need to be a sign. This is back-stage. You should be in the stands."

"No," he says, "I should be in neither of those places. I belong in the ring."

I roll my eyes at the arrogant statement, even though it rings true.

This is a man who would be perfect as a performer. He commands attention just by standing there. He's commanding my attention right now.

"Go ahead." I tell him, "Sasha probably wants a snack."

Something dark flashes across his eyes. "She probably does. That's what you do to the animals, right? You keep them hungry before a performance. Of course, you don't want to go too far. You don't want them *too* hungry. You don't want them to decide that one of the audience members looks more delicious than whatever the trainer's got on a stick."

I shiver. "You don't know anything about us."

"Don't I?" He pushes away from the wall and walks toward me.

I want to back away, but I force myself to stand my ground.

I belong here, he doesn't.

Besides, I can't miss my cue. I don't think my father would actually push me into a ditch, but that's not because of familial love. I'm the headliner for the circus right now. The draw.

The reason why we get even tiny snippets of media in local TV shows when we pass through towns. The great Luna Rider, so much potential, Olympic hopeful…

At least she was a long time ago.

Now she's just a circus sideshow, something to do on an afternoon in a rural town.

The stranger circles me, watching far too close for comfort, his dark eyes taking in everything from my hair in its tight bun to my leotard, my stockings and my bare feet. And they aren't pretty feet. They're the feet of a dancer, of an athlete. They're feet that were cut time after time on tight ropes when I was just little.

The audience can't see them, so it doesn't matter that I can't cover them up with ballet shoes or something else in order to do my act.

This man sees them.

He seems to notice every cut and bump and scar.

He meets my eyes. "I do know you," he says, his voice low, so low.

I almost don't notice how close he is. Not until his breath brushes my temple, warm and almost soothing. In contrast to his words.

"I see that they keep *you* a little hungry too. That you're strong, muscular, but not as much as you should be. Not for someone who works out ten hours a day. That's because they keep you hungry, isn't it? You wake up hungry, you perform hungry, and you go to sleep hungry."

A full body shiver racks me, confirming his words even as I want to deny them.

Yes. My father trained me the same way he trained the animals.

And the worst part, the reason why I can't even condemn him, is that it works. He wanted to build something to revive his flailing circus.

He worked at it and now he has it.

I remember when we would only draw a handful of people when I was a child. They were more concerned with drinking and fighting in the stands than watching the show.

Now, our biggest tent packs 100 people a night, even more if my father can sell the tickets, the fire marshal's rules be damned.

"I'm serious," I say, my voice unsteady. "You shouldn't be back here. The owner of the circus will be upset if he finds you."

"And then what?" he says. "Will he kick me out of the circus? No refunds, right?"

"Right."

"Is that what you want?" He circles me again. And from behind, he leans down, his words soft, his lips moving against my neck. My entire body wakes up, that's the only way to explain it. It comes alive. After nineteen years of sleep, I thought my body was only good for one thing— performing, doing what other people want to see. But this reaction that runs through me, it has nothing to do with being seen. It has to do with feeling the warmth of him behind me, the strength and size of him. A contrast to the softness of his mouth.

He kisses his way up toward my ear.

I should be offended.

I should be horrified.

I should turn around and slap him.

Except then everyone would hear us.

The audience might look over.

The show would stop.

My father would definitely find out.

So I stand very still.

At least, that's the excuse I give myself as I allow his teeth to gently grab my earlobe and tug. It feels like there's a direct path to between my legs.

My nipples turn hard, visible beneath the leotard.

They're barely there, my breasts.

I didn't develop much when I went into puberty. I've always been relatively flat, which served me well when it comes to acrobatics. It's almost like I haven't had breasts until right now, until this moment, when suddenly they've decided to make themselves known. And I want nothing more than for his long-fingered, elegant, masculine hands to be on them.

"What are you doing?" I ask.

"Introducing myself," he murmurs. "It's so very nice to meet you."

The audience laughs, reminding me that I need to be on stage in about 30 seconds.

It's almost my cue.

There's no stage director back here to point it out. I'm just supposed to know, and I always do. No stage director, which means there's no one to see when his hand comes around, splays over my stomach and tugs me back so I can feel him hard and thick against my ass.

"I think I'm going to be seeing a lot of you, Luna Rider," he whispers.

I whirl to face him. "No, you're not."

"I am if you accept my job offer."

An offer of sex. In exchange for things. Money. A car, maybe. Men like him have money. You can tell from his clothes. His confidence. My cheeks flush, because I liked him touching me a little too much. When I thought he wanted me. When I thought he *saw* me, not a body he could purchase as easily as a ticket on the tilt-a-whirl. "No, thanks."

"You don't even want to hear it?" he asks.

"There is *nothing* you could say that could tempt me."

"I don't know," he muses. "I've said so many alluring things."

"Please leave." Agitation makes me twitch. "*Leave.*"

And then, miraculously, he does.

He turns and walks away.

Thank God, I tell myself, pretending I'm glad the alluring stranger is gone.

He can only cause trouble.

Nothing good ever comes from strangers or townies or men for that matter.

I look down.

My nipples are still hard. There's still a warmth and maybe even a slight dampness between my legs. How is it possible that someone could do that in only a few minutes? What is his name? How did he know mine? Maybe he's some kind of Olympics superfan.

He saw an article or a blog post on the local news station and decided to come say hello in a very inappropriate way. With a proposition. An offer of money for sex.

Well, if that's the case, it should be over soon.

It should be over now.

As long as he doesn't go to my father next. I shiver again, and this time it's desire tinged with fear. Somehow that only makes me hotter.

I hear the announcer boom over the speakers indicating that Sasha the beautiful orange-and-black striped tiger is off the stage, along with the rest of the animals and the handler. "And now the amazing Luna Rider soars through the air. Give her a glorious welcome."

I snap into action and run as fast as I can. With every beat of my heart, I run.

There's a trapeze waiting for me down low, reachable. It only takes a small hop, and then I'm on it soaring, soaring through the air, allowing myself to turn and tumble, falling and catching, falling and catching.

This is the one place where I control what happens.

This is the only place in my life where I'm free.

Want to read more? Order BLUE MOON now!

Books by Skye Warren

Endgame Trilogy & more books in Tanglewood
The Pawn
The Knight
The Castle
The King
The Queen
Escort
Survival of the Richest
The Evolution of Man
Mating Theory
The Bishop

North Security Trilogy & more North brothers
Overture
Concerto
Sonata
Audition
Diamond in the Rough
Silver Lining
Gold Mine
Finale

Rochester Trilogy & more
Private Property
Strict Confidence
Best Kept Secret
Hiding Places
Behind Closed Doors

Chicago Underground series
Rough
Hard
Fierce
Wild
Dirty
Secret
Sweet
Deep

Stripped series
Tough Love
Love the Way You Lie
Better When It Hurts
Even Better
Pretty When You Cry
Caught for Christmas
Hold You Against Me
To the Ends of the Earth

The Modern Fairy Tale Duet
Beauty and the Professor
Falling for the Beast

Hughes Series
One for the Money
Two for the Show
Three to Get Ready

**For a complete listing of Skye Warren books,
visit**

www.skyewarren.com/books

About the Author

Skye Warren is the bestselling author of dangerous romance such as the Endgame trilogy. Her books have been on the New York Times, the USA Today, and the Wall Street Journal bestseller lists. They feature powerful men and the strong women who bring them to their knees. She makes her home in Texas with her loving family, sweet dogs, and flying squirrel.

Sign up for Skye's newsletter:
skyewarren.com/newsletter

Like Skye Warren on Facebook:
facebook.com/skyewarren

Join Skye Warren's Dark Room reader group:
skyewarren.com/darkroom

Follow Skye Warren on Instagram:
instagram.com/skyewarrenbooks

Visit Skye's website for her current booklist:
skyewarren.com/books

Copyright

This is a work of fiction. Any resemblance to actual persons, living or dead, business establishments, events or locales is entirely coincidental. All rights reserved. Except for use in a review, the reproduction or use of this work in any part is forbidden without the express written permission of the author.